Butterfly
R·I·S·I·N·G

TANYA WRIGHT

ISBN: 1453650369

ISBN-13: 9781453650363

Library of Congress Control Number: 2010909204

...and a *special* thanks to:

Sherry Huber
Gilda Squire
Wil Colom
the team at CreateSpace
Doris Jean Austin
Roxy Maronyan
the Indian man I met at the Mongolian Bbq
who told me things I'll never tell

My family

The beauty and grace of the butterfly is legendary. The Greeks of the ancient world believed that a person's soul left the body after death and formed itself into a butterfly. The life cycle of the butterfly is known as the complete metamorphosis. It has four distinct, transformative stages during its short life span:

EGG
the roundish reproductive body produced by
the female of certain animals,
according to species

CHAPTER 1

HONEY CHILE SAT PERCHED ATOP THE WEATHERED MILK CRATE like a hen. Her thighs were open just wide enough for a thin stream of air to pass between. She was hot. Honey was a member of the Lucasville Country Chorus, a gregarious group of three (including her husband Pop-Pop and his ace boon coon, Dice) who had little else better to do than to talk about the folks passing by. But Honey Chile clucked for more than just sport. She never told anybody this, but she made up stories in her mind about the people that passed by, where they'd been and what shores they were on their way to. They always turned out to be dead ends, as lives always are, but the spaces before the One Final Moment were always filled with exotic adventures—mostly of love. No one would have guessed the thoughts Honey Chile had about love. Oh! No one. Especially not Pop-Pop.

Those dried leaves mixed with blood weren't working. Ruthie told Honey that was all she had to do—mix a little bit in his food—to get Pop-Pop off her at night. Lately, he was frisky as a bear, and Honey Chile just couldn't stand it. Couldn't get any rest at night on account of him pawing at her like some wild boar. He was taking time away from her quiet—from her made-up stories of the folks she saw pass by. He was pushing up on fifty-eight and was starting to fancy things like sports cars, blue jeans, and hip-talk. Pop-Pop saw his One Final Moment drawing close, so he held on for dear life to the spaces in between. The spaces where he was free and he was a boy, where the living was easy and there were no bills, just the sky and its endless possibilities, no end and no Honey. But what would he have done without Honey? She was the one who, for thirty-three years, set out his clothes every morning and cooked his bacon, fried eggs, and one piece of toast, burnt, just the way he liked it (she started making oatmeal on account of Pop-Pop's high cholesterol report) before they shuffled their feet to the place that had become the center of their lives for the last twenty years—the Country Store.

The store was almost a place riper for clucking than Henry's front porch at Ruthie's Friday night fish fries! My! She saw all types and kinds sidle through. Many were lost, but a lot of city folk came in acting found as they looked around the store and the town, breathing them in and calling them "quaint." Honey had lived in Lucasville all her life; she had never taken a plane anywhere. Planes were part of her dreams—hell, they weren't for life. Not *real* life. This was life: dusty dirt getting swept up by the passing cars, where she had to clean the tops of cans every Wednesday to make sure people didn't start saying her stuff was old. Lucasville was filled to the brim with dust, a red-brown dust that seemed to come from deep inside the earth. No one knew why it was the way it was. Ruthie told her to take some Lucasville dust and mix it in that cup of hers, that cup for Pop-Pop, 'cause it was "special." Special dust, right here in Lucasville! Honey couldn't believe her ears. *Lucasville is a special place with special dust?*

Honey Chile laughed and laughed so hard, that she could feel the air expanding in her jolly ol' belly. Her greasy hair gleamed in the sun as she threw her head back, revealing a half set of crooked, wooden-like teeth: they were wooden on account of her not getting enough vitamins and minerals when she was a babe, at least that's what the doctors told her. She tried hard not to show her teeth when she smiled, but sometimes she forgot herself and those teeth came shining through. Honey laughed out loud and for the few shining moments she did, she was happy, but the joy came like a fume and then vanished, staying just long enough to rile the hope in her.

CHAPTER 2

IT WAS ALMOST SEVEN O'CLOCK AND THE ROOSTER HAD JUST finished doing his thing, his morning cock-a-doodle-do. Rose was tired. The pain in her low back was now at an all-time high, and she could take it no more. Probably the way she slept last night. *That so-and-so was all over me like a cheap suit. No, like white on rice! He was closer than two coats of paint!* She laughed to herself. Rose's laugh was different from Honey's—it was deep and throaty, almost like a man's. Her mama always said she was a woman who acted like a man but looked like liquid sex. Twenty-one years ago, when she was thirteen and the fried eggs on her chest were starting to rise like yeast, her mama tried to keep Rose in the house as much as possible. Rose remembered the day she had power, power over the men folks.

She was playing double Dutch in the middle of the road— just like she always did—and there was Bobby coming down the road. He spotted Rose hurling her body left and right with the jump rope, while the braided ropes on her head bobbed from side to side. Rose was a girl, but she was always a woman inside.

She felt it, and now she saw that Bobby had seen the woman in her, too. It was out. She kept turning rope, but she watched him as he watched her, slowing down almost to a stop to take her in. He started with her feet: they were covered by dirty sneakers, so his eyes didn't rest too long there. He wanted to get to the flesh, and the flesh he did, letting his eyes linger a little too long on the supple legs made strong by months of softball and sports. His eyes rested square on her crotch, held tighter by too-short shorts. The shirt tied at the waist exposed just a thin line of flesh to make him wonder about what lay deep inside the little girl's loins. Then it was the bosom, the young and tender bosom, the long lean neck, and the face—ah, Rose's face. She was a bit unidentifiable, and he liked that. Mixed. A mutt. Had a lot of Indian in her, and she always wore her long, black hair in braided ropes by her side. She was a stunning child—beautiful. Bobby finally came to a dead stop. The girl in the middle stopped jumping, looked at Rose, and then looked at Bobby.

"Evening," he said with a sly smile. He looked squarely at Rose—didn't seem to notice anyone else.

"Evening." Rose looked back at him, part invitation and part challenge. She felt contempt rising up in her for him looking at her that way, but she also felt a sense of power whose surge she would—from this day forward—find almost too intoxicating to ever completely give up. The way Bobby looked at her confirmed her deepest fears about herself, who she was, and what she would become. Bobby tipped his hat and the other little girls watched him saunter off and wondered why he was touching his member as he did.

There was that pain again. It was getting worse and worse, traveling to spaces and nooks she never knew existed in her whole entire body. Just settling in, like it had found a home in her, like it was never gonna leave. When Sarah Mae Brown socked her in the eye for taking her Petey from her, Rose was unmoved. She didn't squirm at all, not a grimace. Nothing. She felt the pain—it hurt like hell—but damned if she was ever going to let them see her cry. Mama used to say she couldn't trust a woman who wouldn't cry from pain. Mama said a lot of things about her that hurt her deep, deep inside, but she never would let on. She never understood these things because she was just being herself. Rose always thought if the world saw her pain, it would have a point of entry and destroy her. Rose's stone-faced ways were really a survival technique; she taught it to herself and mastered it as she became older. But something was changing. Now that she was thirty-four, it was more and more difficult to bear, this stone-facedness, and at times she almost found herself in a heap of tears. She was terrified that, one day, she would just snap and they would see her, they would all see her cry, and then the real brutality would begin.

Being herself was a thing that Rose felt not too many people understood, especially Honey Chile. Rose sighed as she made her way to the rickety door of the Country Store. *Dunno why she just doesn't fix that thing,* Rose thought. The screen door. All manner of flies and dust came through that store, and for just sixty-nine cents, Pop- Pop could buy a yard of screen that would prevent the weekly dusting Honey did with her cans. But it seemed like Honey wanted more work than she could handle, like it was keeping her away from doing something else.

"Morning, Honey." Rose was aware of her voice because it was the first time she had used it this morning. It was always deep, but right now it was even deeper than usual and betrayed her whereabouts the previous evening. She left before last night's Mr. so-and-so had a chance to rise again. She slipped out in the dark of the morning dew and decided to walk her way home, walk and think. She was a thinker like a man, her mama used to say, not a feeler like a woman. "Something is wrong with Rose," she'd say. She had lived her life feeling this way about herself, the way her mama felt about her, but she couldn't be any other way about herself, could only be herself. That was what she knew and who she knew to be, but it was never right. Nothing Rose did was ever quite right in her mama's eyes. It was a fight she stopped wanting to win, and the minute she did, she felt a weight lift off her tiny shoulders. She left her mama's house, never to return again. It was shortly after the exchange she shared with Bobby playing double Dutch, when she had more than a notion about who she was. She found herself being ogled by men and women alike. Rose sometimes felt like she was in a freak show. She was *so* different. She wanted them to like her—but they couldn't. They wouldn't. She went on this way with the world outside of her, happy to be apart and distant from it, yet wanting to be close, closer than those two coats of paint. Or the white on the rice.

Honey Chile was the personification of everything that a woman like Rose Johnson hated: a woman who lived her own life without apologies or complaints. Honey looked at Rose with not-so-veiled contempt, but to be sure, it was mixed with more than a healthy dose of awe and pure and utter admiration. Rose was, in fact, all the things that Honey never had the courage to be. Honey wondered how a woman like Rose could walk the earth with such abandon, like she owned the joint.

"Mornin'," Honey mumbled back to Rose under her breath. She watched as Rose, in her wrinkled dress of scarlet, sashayed herself down the aisle and bent over just so to pick up a container of milk. Rose knew she was being watched by Honey, so she lingered long enough so that Honey could get a proper look at her ass. Both men and women alike had a fascination with her bountiful derriere. She peeked back and saw Honey leaning over to get a better view, so she wiggled her butt for punctuation and then stood up and turned, slow, so Honey could get a view of her front. When Honey's eyes met Rose's, she looked away quickly, hot with shame. Rose put the milk on the counter.

"How much for the milk?"

"Two and fifty."

Rose went for her bosom and took out a wad of money. She peeked up at Honey, whose eyes widened as big as plates. She smiled to herself and then, finally, found a lone five-dollar bill and handed it to Honey.

"Keep the change."

"I don't want your change. It ain't good here."

Honey rang her up and then threw the two fiddy back at her. Rose looked at the money on the counter and then back at Honey. For the first time, Rose noticed the tiny, micro lines about the woman's eyes that were less from age than from sheer and utter weariness. Honey was tired, and she could tell: Rose recognized the look. Only Honey wasn't tired from late nights with men, but from having dreams of love and sugar plums dancing in her head keeping her awake as she chased thoughts that would never be made real.

"Okay then, Honey."

The change was a peace offering. She thought that if Honey took the money, she would also accept the part of Rose she held in such contempt and admiration. But she didn't. So Rose took the money and clutched it tight in her hand. When she walked out of the store—with her wrinkled red dress and her bottle of milk—she released her hand and let the change fall to the ground. Somebody would find it and take it, she hoped.

Quiet as a mouse, Rose slipped into the house. The heel tap for her shoe had broken off, so there was no shield between the nail in her shoe and the cold, wooden floor. *Click, clack, click,* went the shoe heel. That and the rustling of the paper bag with the milk was enough to summon for Grace. She was up anyway, and when Rose felt in the dark for the light switch, little Grace was standing there in her pink ruffled robe, waiting. Pouting. The two locked eyes.

"I been waiting up all night for you, Rose Ma. Where you been?" Grace asked. Rose looked at the little girl.

"Do you know how old I am?" To Grace, it was an odd question. The little girl searched her brain.

"I don't know. Maybe—"

"Old enough to know that when a young girl starts sassing a grown woman about the time she comes in at night, she's liable to get her tail whupped." Little Grace put her hands down by her side. "What you got to say to that?'

"Yes, Rose Ma," the little girl mumbled.

"Speak up! Can't hear you!"

"Yes ma'am!" Grace shouted out loud, but respectfully. Rose watched as Grace looked away.

"What did Rose Ma tell you the last time you woke up and found me gone, huh?"

"That if anything happened, I was to go to Miss Ruthie's house."

"Right. That's right. Miss Ruthie'll take care of you. She'll always take care of you." The little girl bowed again, then waited.

"What else? What else did I tell ya?" said Rose.

"That Rose Ma is gonna be all right. That you gonna be okay," Grace said.

"So stop worrying about your Rose Ma, you hear me? What does worrying do?"

"Give you wrinkles..."

"Speak up! Can't hear you!"

"Worrying gives you wrinkles!"

"And we don't want that!" Rose and Grace said this at the same time, as if on cue. It was a ditty they'd clearly memorized, a shared moment between a woman and girl that neither time nor space would ever diminish. Rose buried her face under little Grace's arm, and the sweet smell of fresh rose and baby powder put her at ease. She thought, *Grace is a girl. Grace is such a girl.*

"I love you, Rose Ma." The little girl smoothed Rose's long hair down. She looked into Rose's eyes, searching. Waiting.

Finally, Rose answered. "Ditto."

The little girl was disappointed again. She always got the same response from Rose.

"Time to get ready for school. Now, git!" Rose swatted the girl playfully on the butt and watched as she rushed off to her room to get dressed. Looking down, she saw the yellow ribbon that fell out of Grace's head and tied it to her own. Seeing her reflection in the mirror she smiled, tentatively at first, as if someone were watching, and then more broadly.

Something caught her eye out the window, and in the distance, Rose saw a cloaked woman. She knew it was Ruthie but she didn't call out. She watched as Ruthie bent down and gathered up the dried leaves, mixed them with the earth and the blood, then buried the little bundle underneath the old sycamore tree. When Ruthie turned, Rose moved out of view. Feeling safe, Ruthie gathered herself and rushed off. Rose shook her head, sorry that the woman felt she had to resort to such means and even sorrier about what she was doing in the first place. The truth was, Rose wasn't after Ruth's husband, Henry. Hell, she didn't care about him in the least! That man seemed to have an urge so strong she was just satisfying him, satisfying her. They were all the same, these men. All of them except the one who always stayed on her mind.

Little Gracie emerged from her room, fresh bobby socks, starched dress, and pin curls let loose so her hair fell in cascades that framed her angelic little face. She was sweet but tart, Grace was. Rose had the thought and smiled as she mixed the cornmeal gruel. She tasted it. Too little water? Not enough sugar? Whatever it was, the oatmeal was a hot mess and Rose knew it. She tried to make it right by serving it to little Gracie with a smile. Grace put the meal to her lips and quickly spit it out.

"What's wrong? It needs some sugar." It was a statement, but Rose sounded unsure.

"Have you tasted this, Rose Ma? I don't think sugar can help it."

"Alright now." Rose looked at her sternly, but she looked away quickly so as not to betray the smile in back of her eyes. Gracie was something else, but she always told the truth. Rose couldn't cook worth a damn—never could. Rose could never understand why she had to cook when there were other things she did— things she did real good—that more than compensated for her complete and utter lack of culinary skills.

"Miss Ruthie didn't send no cornbread down from the fry?"

"Oh, as a matter of fact she did. Go look in my pocket."

Grace jumped up, ran to Rose's coat and pulled out a greasy napkin; inside was a wet piece of sweet cornbread. Grace ate it hungrily.

"That ain't no proper breakfast, Grace."

"Neither is that!" Grace pointed to the oatmeal sludge that was slowly but surely turning into a hard, cold rock.

"Time for you to get to school."

"Yes, Rose Ma." Grace rushed over and bent down to get her books. Rose noticed the petticoat beneath her dress and called out as Grace raced toward the door.

"Grace!"

"Yes, Rose Ma?"

"You got a boyfriend?"

"A boyfriend? Yuck! No, Rose Ma! Why you say such an awful thing as that?"

"Just wondering."

"Anyway, I'd tell you if I did. You know that, Rose Ma, don't you?"

"Yes. Yes, I do." Rose hoped she was right. She nuzzled herself into the little girl's armpit again. This time, Grace took out the lone yellow ribbon in her hair and tied it onto Rose's.

"Now you have two!" Grace laughed.

"Gracie, where am I going to go with two yellow ribbons in my head?"

"Anywhere you want, Rose Ma! You don't have to go no-where at all if you don't want. Just walk around the house with 'em on."

Smiling, Grace caressed Rose's face. "I love you, Rose Ma." The little girl waited again, hoping that this time it would be different.

"Ditto."

CHAPTER 3

RUTHIE WAS A HANDSOME, BARREN WOMAN WHO HAD LOST MORE children than she could count. When she miscarried baby number sixteen, she promised herself she would never try to get pregnant again, but she broke the promise almost immediately after she made it. She didn't understand this impulsive desire to get pregnant, lose a baby, then get pregnant again. She took no time to grieve in between the bouts. Sixteen plus times a baby came sooner than her body could make them. She knew that grief gone unchecked could do harm to the griever, but that didn't stop her from pushing her feelings deeper into herself to make the next baby. Ruthie said that she'd had so many half-formed ravaged babies slip out of her womb that she never knew their names or saw their faces, so she never had any connection to them. This was a complete lie. There was a bond she had with each and every one of those children—she named every one—before she put them in a box or flushed them down a toilet bowl.

Ruthie married Henry when she was sixteen. Henry was eighteen. He was taking over his father's automotive business and needed a wife to help him and Ruthie was there. Henry needed Ruthie, but not in the ways she wanted.

Henry was barrel-chested with short, skinny legs. He liked to keep his mass of curls greased down and parted to the side. He, Pop-Pop and Dice had gone the way of middle age now, and Henry bought a 1955 Chevy pickup truck that he fancied more than just about anything else in the whole wide world. He'd get up early in the morning and oil that thing, rubbing it with a grease rag until his hands were blistered, black and blue. It was his saving grace, that truck. Something about the oil between his fingertips took him to a lighter time in his life, a time when he wasn't bogged down by a wife unable to keep a baby in her stomach. A time when the living was free and easy.

Now that the laying and the loving was less and less frequent, he fantasized about Rose while he was in bed beside his wife at night. He couldn't help himself, but there was just something about Rose that had him. He'd hoped that maybe someday Rose would learn to love him, barrel chest and all. He knew he wasn't and never would be as fine as those city slickers she always had on her arm, but maybe there was a part of her—some tiny part—that had pity on a man like him and she would learn to love him.

Suddenly, one day it happened. Rose was at the bus stop and it was raining. She looked so beautiful, her black silken hair matted down and her wet, too-tight dress stuck to her body in a way that made the most erotic picture in his mind. He was in his truck and he could help her—he could take her to her destination and get her out of the rain! For one shining moment, he felt needed. If he could help a woman like Rose Johnson in her time of need, there wasn't nothing he couldn't do.

He had come to live for his wife's Friday night fish fries where Rose would sometimes show up. Henry was always waiting in anticipation of seeing Rose's face. Sometimes she would come on time, like the others, and stand holding up a corner, looking around at the sorry lot of them. The other Lucasville women huddled around on the opposite side, clucking and talking about women things, but mostly about Rose. Rose didn't seem to mind, didn't seem to care. When the others were kicking back moonshine and ripple, Rose nursed a Ball jar of sweet tea the whole night through—that is, if she stayed the whole night. She rarely did, and Henry wondered why Rose even came when the women treated her so bad. But the men didn't. Men didn't ever treat Rose Johnson bad. The few who had the courage to talk to her always fell at a heap by her feet, ready to go with her wherever she went, do whatever she said.

Henry beeped his horn when he saw her. She heard him, but she stayed her gaze looking ahead, to see if the bus's headlights would come to deliver her. He beeped again.

Lord, if this man don't leave me alone, she thought, then sighed. She turned to meet his gaze. She could see him plain because he had rolled the window down so she could get a good view. He smiled—hopeful, willing, waiting—and opened the truck door, urging her to come inside. Finally, she put one sexy, high-heeled foot in front of the other and walked to a waiting Henry in his 1955 truck.

The inside of the truck was bigger than she thought and smelled of oil. At first he seemed scared—like he didn't know what to do now that the woman of his dreams was finally with

him in his truck. Here. Alone. He had rescued her from the wind
and the rain. She looked at him, expectant.

"Ain't you gonna drive?"

"Anywhere you want! Where you going to, Rose?" She just
looked at him. He wanted her so bad she could smell it. So she
offered herself to him and he took her, hungrily and without
an ounce of restraint. When they were through, Henry was a
changed man. A look of calm—serene bliss—had overtaken
him. He was quiet and contemplative and stole a portion of his
weekly earnings to give the front desk at the best hotel two towns
over just so he could have Rose. He was head over heels for this
woman and he would leave his wife for her if she just said the
word. "Yes, Rose, say yes!"

He uttered this mantra in his sleep as he lay beside his awake
wife.

He had no idea he was revealing all in his dreams, his secret
life of fantasy. Middle-aged men spend more time daydreaming
and fantasizing than any group of people alive—there was a
study on it in the *Lucasville Record*, the local paper. Henry found
himself in the men they quoted in the article, and it gave him a
feeling of peace. There was—in fact—a name for what he was
feeling. But when he was with Rose, he didn't feel the longing or
the aching anymore. The moment before he came—and it was
always sooner than he would have liked—all was right with the
world and he was young again, but only when he was with Rose.
Yes, Rose Johnson had a spell over all men, but nothing like the
one she had over Henry. He would move mountains for her if
she asked, fly to the moon for her if she looked like that's what
she wanted him to do. But she never did. She didn't know why

she let this man inside her every week; it was just that he seemed to need her so badly.

Ruthie knew about it all—and that's why she was mixing the blood and the leaves with the earth and putting it beneath Rose's ol' weeping willow—to run her out of town, to keep Rose away from Henry. But her concoctions weren't working. Why? Ruthie was the one everybody called when their child was sick with colic or if they wanted a man's attention. She told them the types of herbs and potions to mix and she was helping others to fulfill their dreams. Sometimes she felt that if she could help give people what they wanted, she could fulfill her own destiny. But most times she just wanted to stop Rose from laying with her husband.

"She ain't got no scrupulous, Ruthie," Honey Chile told her as Ruthie lay crying in her lap one day. "She got a hold on a man I ain't nevah seen before. What about your potions, sugah? Ain't they working?"

"No. Ain't nothing working. And I done tried everything."

"What she need is a good old-fashioned beat down is all. Me and the girls can get her in a corner and just beat her little ass!" Honey waved her tiny chocolate fists in the air. "Wouldn't be no problem, Ruthie. Wouldn't be no problem at all."

Ruthie waved her arm. "Thanks Honey, but I got to fight my own battles. The one raging inside me is the one only I can win."

"Or lose," said Honey, as she shook her head and sucked her teeth, itching for a fight just to take the edge off.

CHAPTER 4

LOOPY LITTLE LILAH AWOKE FROM UNDERNEATH THE KITCHEN table and she wasn't sure how she got there. Her head hurt. Baby was curled up in a fetal position right next to her, quiet as a lamb. She wore candy-striped tights with polka-dot dresses, always looking as if she were in some perennial arrested development, her stringy blond hair, blue eyes, and rosy cheeks vestiges of the child who still lived within the thirty-three-year-old woman. If Rose, Honey, and Ruthie were women who had dreams, Lilah would be the one who lived them. She was inventive in devising them, too. She spent countless hours on the details of her schemes. "Little things mean a lot," she told Ruthie one day, as if she had thought of the oft-used phrase on her own. Things just came out of Lilah like that. She was very much like a child—like the way she tilted her head when someone told her a story because she was imagining it as she went along. She tilted herself so that she could see it better. A head upright is one that can't enjoy the view, but one tilted to the side—ah, yes, you could see through the looking glass like Alice in Wonderland and see all there is to see. And more.

Lilah wanted to sing—and she did, a long time ago, long before she married Samuel. Samuel was seventy when they married and he wanted a woman he could die with so he picked Lilah. On their wedding day, he promised he would turn her loose if she ever changed her mind about him, set her free like a sprightly little butterfly and let her spread her wings. Her kiss was the acceptance of the out he gave her in their marriage contract. Lilah was spending her days and nights being a dutiful wife when Nat found Baby Girl, an injured dog, almost dead in a ditch. Lilah nursed the dog back to health with daily runs, food, and love. Samuel was indifferent to her ever-present companion, but Baby loved him anyway. Samuel would reach down every so often and sneak Baby a beef bone to show he cared. He never let Lilah see him do it, but she knew that he did. Baby had buried a whole mess of them in the backyard.

Lilah always seemed to be dancing inside. She wanted to sing, yeah, but she wanted to dance, too. She did it in public sometimes, much to the chagrin of the others, but they had learned to accept the girl's ways. Strange, a little odd, yes, but she wasn't threatening, and she always seemed to be in a state where she needed to be taken care of, and so they did. Take care of Lilah, that is. These days, she needed it more than ever because she was moments away from hurting herself, and it all started the day Nat died.

It was a crisp Sunday afternoon about a year earlier. She had just come from the market and got some overripe peaches to make a pie. She and Nat lived together in their dead mama's house, and they didn't have anyone else in the world but each other. Lilah knew that the folks in Lucasville thought there was something strange about a grown-up brother and sister living together like that in the same house, but she didn't care. Her brother loved her, and she sure as hell loved Nat. He was a handsome, strapping sort with ruddy cheeks, blue eyes, and blond hair, just like hers. Only his stayed coiled and close to his head in ringlets.

Nat was good with his hands. He could fix *anything!* What she liked most about her brother was that he never said nothing bad about nobody, even when he knew they were wrong. He just painted a small smile on his face and forgave their transgressions. Lilah admired this most about her brother because she was less able to restrain herself when she was hot. It wasn't often she got angry, but when she did, ooh wee! Nat used to laugh at her when he saw the heat rising in his little sister, and it immediately made her calm. She couldn't get mad when Nat was around—no one did. Something about him just wouldn't let you, and if you did, you wouldn't stay that way for long.

He had gone to the store 'cause she was out of sugar and she needed it for the pie. He took the keys hanging on the nail by the door, mussed her hair, and gave her a kiss on the cheek. Nat's kisses on the cheek were the sweetest things. She watched out the window as he got into the car, started it up, and made his windy way down to Honey and Pop-Pop's Country Store, down the country road. She smiled. It was a pretty day and the sun was high, high in the sky. Maybe she and Baby Girl would take a walk up the road to visit Ruthie and see what the tea leaves were saying.

They told her that Nat had jumped out to fix Miss Harris's tire when Miss Crenshaw—the old spinster down the road— came flying out of nowhere. Miss Crenshaw had more money than God, yet she still owned the plastic she used to wrap her husband's sandwiches just in case she needed it. He was dead and gone ten years, but she held on just in case there was no more to go around. Miss Crenshaw knew a lot about that—about not having enough.

She didn't see the boy—really, she didn't. She had let go of the guy who used to drive her around because he wanted too much money. He had hiked his rates, she was sure of it, because she left her bank statements out one day. Surely he had seen how much money she had. But he just needed to start saving for his expanding family and he had driven for Miss Crenshaw thirteen years without a single raise. Everybody said she was as cheap as could be, but he didn't care as long as he got paid what he felt he was worth. And he felt he was worth a lot more than he was getting so that, with the need to feed another baby on the way, he asked for his due. And she fired him.

Now she was driving her car on her own. She was ninety-six, and of course, she shouldn't have been driving at all. The few who gave a damn about her offered to get her groceries, her medicine and take her to the doctor, but she always refused, thinking their real motive was to get inside her pocketbook, which she guarded with her life. When her car hit Nat, they said he died instantly. The police came, then the morgue wagon took him away. Miss Crenshaw didn't even get out of the car.

His body was perfectly intact when Lilah saw him at the funeral home. There wasn't no family to speak of, so it was just her, Lilah, alone now without her Nat. He was gone. To her, all the goodness of the world had gone along with him.

At first, Lilah started the drinking to relieve the pain. Then the urge to do it came on faster and stronger, so she resorted to keeping a little flask tied around the inside of her thigh, like a garter belt. That way, she always had a swig when she needed it. Drink or no, though, Lilah still found herself in the strangest predicaments after Nat died, ones she couldn't explain. Like why she was huddled under the dining room table, how she got there and what time she fell asleep. These watery, hazy stages of prolonged blackness set off spells that would carry her so deep inside herself, she didn't know which way was up—or how she got there or how to get out.

Yes, she did know a way out. She could see it in the light when the spirits called; she felt closest to the spirits when she was sleeping or drunk, so she tried to be one or the other as often as possible. It was the light where Nat was, but it was shining bright, and if she got too close to it, she—an alive human being—might get burned and die. But death was what she wanted for herself because if she were dead, she would be where Nat was. *Oh, Nat!* Sometimes Lilah's call for Nat was so loud and so strong, she could feel her baby brother in the center of her chest, rising, rising like a butterfly ready to spread his wings and fly. The more the butterfly rose in her chest, the farther and farther away Lilah got from reality and the closer to the center of her dreams. That was where Nat lay, in the light with her dreams and the butterflies flying high in the sky.

It was where she longed to be, with Nat, but something was grounding her, rooting her to the earth. *It is not your time to die,* the spirits said, but Lilah was insistent. Her flirtation with the light caused her breathing to slow down, almost to a stop; her eyes rolled back in her head, and she felt her body get cold, all the life and blood rushing out to wherever life and blood rushes to when you're dying. Everything audible was far away, getting farther still, when she got closer to the light. It was peaceful there. Nat and the butterflies were there, and if she could just touch it, get a taste, she could feel her brother. That's what she wanted most, to feel him. She had resolved within herself that she would never see him again. *There are many ways to see,* said the spirits. *Don't always believe your eyes.* She listened and they heard her, her desire to be with her brother, but the job of the spirits is not to judge but to obey, obey our needs, wishes and wants, and so they answered by bringing her closer to the light. Lilah was dying and she was happy. But there was a struggle in her to live—sometimes she didn't know what part of her would win the war. And when there was The Black—the black from the light she saw only when she was drunk or asleep—she simply didn't care.

The house was a mess after a bout of the Black Light. One day after Nat died, Lilah celebrated her brother's birthday with a birthday cake, plus some candles and a curly lock of Nat's baby hair wrapped in a ribbon. Lilah lay on the floor remembering how lovely Nat's hair was: blond tufts so soft and light they made him look almost like a girl. He was pretty even as he lay stiff in the casket. He looked like he had when he kissed her cheek and left her to get the sugar for the peach pie. Drunk, she crawled on all fours toward the table; Baby Girl perked up. She poured herself into the too-small chair and then poured herself a cup of tea. She lifted Baby Girl and stuffed the dog into the other chair, then put birthday hats on them both. She took a tiny teaspoon and clinked the cup, lifting it high in the air. She was unsteady.

"Happy birthday to you! Happy birthday to you! Happy birthday dear Nat, happy birthday to you!" Lilah sang. Baby girl howled at the moon and the light from the candle. Lilah's voice was sure, strong, and melodic. When Lilah sang, her whole body sang with her. Time stood still to hear the voice that sounded so different from the body it came out of. It was a strong, sure and powerful voice from a woman who appeared to be fragile and frail.

Lilah lifted her cup to the heavens, then reached down to take out the flask tied to her thigh and emptied it into the cup. Lilah was already drunk. Unbeknownst to her, she had been drunk every day since Nat died, and it was nearing on almost five months the day she gave him that birthday party.

Samuel smelled the liquor on her, but for some reason it was easier for him to say Lilah was crazy. He said she was always crazy, but now she was even crazier since her brother went away. Wasn't nothing he could do for his young bride but try and love her the best he could. Before Nat died, Lilah was a spirited and enthusiastic lovemaker, whispering sweet things and naughty nothings in his ear when she rode him like a cowgirl. It was a good life he had with Lilah—by his accounts, a great one. But after Nat died, Lilah receded so much that she wasn't too sure how she was feeling about anything. She made him nervous sometimes, like she was gonna ask for that clause in their contract one day soon. He resolved to hold onto her as tight as he could for as long as he could. If he'd learned anything all his years on this earth, he'd learned he had to live for today, because anything could happen tomorrow. "God has a plan. It just ain't yours," he said to himself. After he said it, he always sighed, shook his head, and shuffled along.

A few days after Nat's birthday party, Lilah went to see Ruthie. Lilah looked deep inside her cup like she was trying to find something. Then, suddenly, excitedly, she screamed:

"Ruthie!"

Ruthie was looking in her cup of leaves, deep in thought. "Lilah," Ruthie whispered and hung her head down low. She said her name like an exhalation, but it wasn't a breath filled with ease, peace, or relaxation. She looked deeper and deeper.

"How you been, buttercup?"

"Fine, just fine." Lilah waved away a fly that wasn't there. She was unsteady. Ruthie just looked at her.

"How long we been knowing each other, Lilah?"

"Oh, I don't know. Near about fifteen years, I guess," Lilah said.

"You been a friend. A good friend indeed." Ruthie never for a second took her eyes off of Lilah. Ruthie took her hand.

"I see you. See you in the tea." Ruthie said it straight, no chaser. Lilah laughed uncomfortably. She waved again at the air, at the imaginary fly—a butterfly?—in the air.

"You know I don't believe in that stuff, Ruthie." She laughed again. "But tell me—tell me true: what do the leaves say?" Ruthie leaned in.

"Sugar, you ain't wrapped too tight," Ruthie said.

"I could have told you that, Ruthie! Ha!" The discomfort in her laugh grew louder, stronger and more insistent, like a beast about to burn.

"The leaves say you need a healing. You ain't got much time before you—"

"How's Henry doing, Ruthie? You and Henry?" Lilah blurted out the attack and hated herself for it, but she needed something—anything—to take the heat off her and put it onto someone else. She felt desperate, like a caged bird with a cat about to strike. She watched Ruthie's face change.

"Dunno. Ask Rose," Ruthie said. Lilah swatted at the air again.

"Don't she got enough men? Why she want to take something don't belong to her?"

"Ain't no use applying logic to a woman like Rose Johnson," Ruthie said.

Lilah just shook her head. "Saw her down at Lula Mae's with this mop-headed city slicker wearing alligator shoes and purple suspenders. He thought he was clean. Mighty good looking, though, with big old diamonds in his ears and around his neck. But I couldn't take my eyes off her skirt! That skirt was so tight I kept staring at her stomach to make sure she was still breathing!" Lilah laughed. She covered her mouth, then fluttered her hands excitedly in the air.

"Henry being with Rose hurts like hell—that sure is true—but I ain't got nothing to worry about. Rose done had many men—hell, she had just about every man in Macon County! But there's only one man that counts. The one that don't want her: Solomon Jones. And he lives in Newhope." Ruthie looked away.

Lilah looked at her for a long moment and thought about how Ruthie had suffered the lives and deaths of many while she was unstable because of the death of just one. She wanted to take the pain away from Ruthie and take it on herself, for the both of them.

Lilah looked at her tea and confessed: "You're right, Ruthie. Something's growing in me. Something wicked and wild."

CHAPTER 5

I<small>T WAS</small> F<small>RIDAY NIGHT AND FOLKS WAS FEELING ALL RIGHT.</small>
Ruthie turned the golden strips of sweet catfish in the hot, hot
grease. The cornbread cooled by the sill, and the lemonade and
the sweet tea were outside, made even sweeter by the sun.

Ruthie was looking at Henry watching the road toward Rose's
house. He was expectant, giddy with the anticipation of seeing
his ladylove. His hair was freshly slicked and he wore his tweed
pants, the ones he wore just for special occasions such as these.
The Friday night fry was a veritable institution in Lucasville, a
place for the Country Chorus to recap the week and plot new
schemes for the coming one. Ruthie turned the fish and rubbed
her stomach. It was chaffed from her rubbing so hard. She rubbed
hard because, lately, it was harder and harder for her to feel her
hands on her belly—it was so numb—so she had to dig deeper
and deeper. *Maybe if I gave Henry a baby, he wouldn't have to go to Rose,*
she thought. *Hell, Rose ain't gonna give Henry no baby,* she thought, so
that argument didn't work in her mind.

Every Friday night before the fry, when she turned the fish over in the hot grease, she thought of ways to keep her husband at home. Seemed nothing she tried worked, including the formerly foolproof tinctures she concocted for all the ills that ailed the world. She had "get out of jail" potions, "get my money back" potions, "make him love me" potions, "good luck, bad luck" potions, "run the spooks out my house" potions, "make the verdict come out in my favor" potions and everything in between. The remedies only worked if the person mixing the potion and the person asking for it *believed*. *Believed* that whatever it is they said they wanted was going to come true—hell, believed it was already so. That was the trick. Or was it? It said plain in the Bible, hear tell, and in every religious book known to man.

She thought about going to see Lazarus. Lazarus of the Butterflies. He lived at the edge of Newhope, a strange, spirit-like man who gardened with his dogs and his butterflies by day and at night came to those who were ready to change after some personal catastrophe—their own personal Black Light—like a lost loved one or a divorce. Some cataclysmic human tragedy that breaks the human spirit into a billion pieces. The Black Light of the human soul emerges, and Lazarus—a human instrument of the spirit guides who live in the air—can come to help discard some pieces and rearrange or re-create the others. They would be held together by a glue-like faith in the form of *belief*, making the pieces better, stronger, badder and bolder than they were before the event that caused the break. *Belief* was a vital and necessary element to the work that Lazarus performed and could *only* be supplied in limitless quantities by the receiver of his special brand of grace.

Lazarus had a telephone-like sense. He would hear a "ring" in his mind and the spirits would come to give him the who, what, where, when and why. Folks told Ruthie to go see Lazarus, said he was the only one who could heal her barren belly and make it moist, ripe and full for the babies to come from inside of her. But Ruthie knew a piece of her didn't believe—mostly that it could be so easy. And so the babies never came. She resigned herself to her fate, but she could never make full and pure peace with it.

Henry looked at his watch. He came back inside the house, tidying up like he was having a first date.

"What time the people coming, Ruthie?"

"Same time they been coming every Friday for the last ten years. Seven thirty." Henry looked at his watch again and then at the setting of the sun, just to be sure. But you can never be too sure. **Don't believe your eyes,** said the spirits. Henry could hear the spirits too sometimes, but mostly he just ignored them. Henry paced his linoleum floor with Rose on his mind. What was she going to wear? What was she going to do? Was she going to come at all?

While Henry was tidying, Rose held court at the local bar as all the men surrounding her did every trick in the book to get her attention. They bored her so, each pickup line worse than the next. She twirled the ice cubes in her empty glass and the bartender came up.

"Another Shirley Temple?"

"Yes, please. Make it a double this time."

"Your wish is my command." The bartender smiled and went to fill Rose's drink. She never touched alcohol. She saw what it did to her family, tore her mama and her daddy apart. Her daddy got drunk so often that, one night, he forgot himself and ended up in her bed. He didn't mean any harm, and she knew it, so she didn't tell anybody about it. But he left his tie in her room and her mama found it the next day and looked at her. Looked at her real mean, like she smelled like shit or something. Rose could never understand that about her mama. She had birthed Rose, sure, but she never seemed to want to lay any claims to her—never cared about her, held her, loved her or protected her. Whenever Rose did something that didn't look like anybody else, she just clucked her teeth, shook her head and whispered, "The bad seed. That's what she is. I birthed the bad seed!" She began to believe this moniker her mother gave her and so she acted accordingly, thinking that she was "fresh" and "fast" like everybody said. Hell, maybe she was. But she didn't know for sure, and the burden of people thinking they knew who she was was ever-present.

He walked into the bar talking trash. Jacob Barnes was a big-time dealer in Chicago who frequently made stops to Lucasville to visit his ailing mother. But the fistfuls of hundred-dollar bills he stuffed in his mama's hand every month did nothing to heal the pain she felt of a life lived crusading for her people while her son became a drug dealer. He spotted Rose straightaway, as men like Jacob often do with women like Rose. He smiled, licked his lips clean of the taste of the previous woman, then slowly, deliberately, pimp-rolled his way to her.

She offered little more than a scant smile and looked at him with interest. *This guy has a lot of shit with him,* she thought. *I'm bored. Why not have a little fun?* She threw back her double Shirley Temple and turned her body to receive his, letting him get a good look at what he was about to get into. Or what she was about to conquer.

"Hey there, pretty lady. How you?"

"Oh, I'm fine. Just fine."

"I know you fine, but how are you *feeling?*"

Rose smiled. She calculated quickly in her head the number of times she had heard that pickup line. So far, he was coming up short. Empty. Unoriginal. But there was something about him...

"What's your name?"

"Rose. Rose Johnson."

"Rose, I'm Jacob. Jacob Barnes." He took her hand and grazed it oh so gently with his full, luscious lips. She tingled.

"What are you drinking there, pretty Rose?"

"Shirley Temple."

Jacob laughed. "A Shirley Temple?" He took her in with his eyes, looked her body over from the head to the toe. "You gonna be full of surprises, ain't you Rose?"

She rode him like a stallion and he whimpered beneath her like a contented baby who's almost full from the milk from its mama's teat. He was good—real good, better than most. She liked it. She liked him, but she didn't know why. When she looked down at him just as he was about to climax, she had to stifle a chuckle— she didn't know if she was laughing at him or with him. It was that look that men get in their eyes when they're about to come that's the best, the funniest look of all. It's like a roiling volcano rising higher and higher in them, and then, finally, the moment right before the explosion, there's the *thought* of the explosion and then it comes—oh, my! It was that moment that men looked the most vulnerable, and it was in that moment she fucked them harder. She was spent with this one. He had taken a little bit of work, probably 'cause she didn't come far after the other woman he'd had sex with—her estimation was that she was the second in the last twenty-four hours. Rose was an expert. She could do this for the money, good money, but she didn't want to—she considered it charity.

When it was over, he lay in bed and lit a cigarette. He looked at her for a good long time.

"What?" she said coyly, mixed with a hint of indignation.

"You sure is. . .something." He licked her breasts and touched them softly. "Where'd you learn to do the things you do?"

"You don't learn how to make love to a man, you got to feel it," she said. "It ain't no paint-by-the-number situation where you touch his chest, then slowly work your way down to his stomach. You got to know what he wants and give it to him."

He smiled slyly. "What do *you* want, Rose? Any man ever give it to you?"

Rose looked away. Her face got hot. She wasn't expecting that. "As a matter of fact he did." Now she looked at him squarely. She could feel the hot tears rising to the surface, but she was so expert at pushing them down that it hardly took a moment for them to disappear again.

"Is that right?" he asked, sincerely interested. "Well, where is he now?"

"Newhope."

"Newhope! Why ain't you with him?"

She turned the question over and over again in her mind. She had asked the same question a hundred—hell, a million times before. If she came up with a thousand answers, she came up with none.

Solomon.

"Because I ain't, that's why. Any more questions?" He knew right then and there to quit while he was ahead and so he did. Wasn't no reason to put a woman like Rose's mind on anything other than the thing she was expert at. He looked at her, smiled slyly, and started to dive into her bosom for seconds.

She pushed him back. "Not now. I'm hungry."

"Me too, baby." He started for her southern parts.

"I want to eat some food. Real food. The kind you put in your mouth and chew."

Jacob rose, disappointed.

"What you want, baby? I'll take you anywhere you want. Steak? Chicken?"

"Fish. I want fish."

The joint was jumping at Ruthie and Henry's. The whole town was there. Honey Chile, Pop-Pop and Dice took their usual positions with their 411 on all the goings-on. First, it was the news.

"...that man don't know what in the hell he talking 'bout." (Dice)

"Neither do you!" (Pop-Pop!)

"Will y'all shut your traps? Neither one of you know what the tea is on that. I know! You better ask somebody!" (Honey Chile)

There were roars of laughter from the crowd, but Lilah was numb. She was without Samuel—he stopped going to Ruthie's Friday night fries long ago. He was snug as a bug in his bed. "That's what seventy-six years will do to ya," he said with a sigh and a smile. Lilah could get him to go if she wanted to, but she knew he didn't want to, so she didn't. She absentmindedly bit a piece of the fish and burned the roof of her mouth, her tongue and the insides of her cheeks. The burn sobered her up for a moment before the alcohol kicked in and she felt the Black Light turn on inside her. It was becoming more and more familiar, this Black Light, the place she would call home, the place where she felt closest to Nat. She stayed in a corner, propped up by the intersection of two walls.

Henry was pacing, kept looking at the door for Rose, while Ruthie watched Henry. Someone started with a banjo, another a harmonica, until there was a virtual band in the center of Ruth's living room. Folks took turns, Ruthie kept turning the fish, Henry kept pacing and Honey Chile and the chorus kept clucking. Dice stated strumming on his old banjo.

"I need somebody to sing me a song, sing me a song and carry me along. . ." Dice was a bad singer and an even poorer lyricist. The crowd laughed. He turned to Lilah.

"Lilah Belle! Come on, sing us a song!"

"Dice, you know I don't sing no more."

"Lilah! Sing. Us. A. Song!" The crowd hushed.

She looked around the room at all the expectant eyes. Finally, she closed her eyes, tilted her head back, and pushed forth a song.

"I, I got something on my mind, and I, I won't take up too much time, and I, I just got to let you know, so listen, here it goes…"

The crowd dulled to a low hush. The song was haunting and inspired awe. Lilah sang as if the whole room's eyes weren't on her—so free in herself, in her body. It was like she was in the comfort and safety of her home all alone, and she was. She was home with a song—you could tell. Probably more at home than anytime or anywhere else. When Lilah sang the last note, the crowd stopped slowly—they waited to see if there was any more honey to come out of that thin, pink mouth of Lilah Belle's, if there was any more song.

"*Rose!*" Henry yelped like a dog when she came through the door with Jacob. Ruthie turned away in shame—she didn't know if she was more embarrassed for herself or for her husband.

"How you doing? We got hot catfish, collard greens, macaroni and cheese, sweet cornbread—" Henry noticed Jacob, and then, just like that, his heart fell through the floorboards. He knew he couldn't compete with this younger, finer, worldly city slicker. "Peach cobbler, monkey bread, and jambalaya…" By now, everyone—including Jacob—had caught on to Henry's disappointment with his presence.

Jacob smiled a huge, wide grin. "Sounds great! Where the plates at?"

"Ain't no more," Honey said tersely, pursing her lips in the air. Pop-Pop nudged her. Ruthie handed Jacob a plate. No matter who he was or who brought him, Jacob was a guest in her home and he would be treated with the respect all guests deserve and received under her roof.

"Sure. Sure. Just help yourself." Dejected, Henry slumped away.

"Look like he already has," Ruthie said under her breath, as she gave Rose a cool once-over and followed her husband into the house.

Lilah had seen it all from the upstairs window. She looked a long while at Rose and noticed...something. Perhaps it was the way she held her plate in the form of a request, jutting it out. The plate was empty, and the gesture made Rose look vulnerable. She shook herself. "That woman hurt my Ruthie," she said to herself. "I got no right seeing the good in her." *Don't believe your eyes,* she heard the spirits warn her. Honey Chile followed Ruthie and Henry, to console or incite. Lilah followed with her eyes, then with her heart and, finally, she went away from the window.

Rose and Jacob ate heartily, and it was good. Ruthie sure did know how to cook! Rose always admired that about Ruthie, how well she could cook and keep a home. She wished sometimes her mind could get stayed on such things, but she just didn't seem to have it in her. She finished her food, took Jacob's, and threw both soggy paper plates in the trash.

"I'm going to go freshen up," she said. Rose took her bag and started toward the bathroom upstairs.

Lilah looked around—she was in Ruthie's tea room. It was a room unlike any other in the house: a hodge-podge of assorted pictures and records, Ruthie read her tea leaves from a silver tea set in a corner. Lilah spotted a shadowbox with a dead butterfly in it and picked it up.

"Got that shadowbox from Lazarus." Ruthie turned to Lilah. "You should see Lazarus. He can heal you, Lilah."

Honey Chile entered, just as nosy as can be. "Aw, shit! You ain't talking about 'Lazarus of the Butterflies,' are you? That man live over in Newhope with them dawgs and them butterflies following him everywhere? The man who can heal you and make all your dreams come true? Is that who you mean, Ruthie?" Honey Chile asked.

Ruthie nodded.

"Yes."

"Well, I'll be damned. I'll be damned!" Honey Chile hit her plump thigh.

Ruthie turned to Lilah and looked at her pointedly. "You still young, Lilah. Leave Samuel. You still young, still got your looks and a whole life ahead of you. Don't stay here to die in Lucasville—you got too much life in you."

"How am I going to get to Newhope? I ain't got no car," Lilah asked. She was surprised the question came out of her so fast.

"I'll give you mine. I'll give you Henry's truck." Ruthie and Lilah looked at each other for a long moment. It was settled between them, just like that.

Honey Chile waved her hands in the air as if she were in church with the Holy Ghost. "Henry's truck? *Henry's truck!* That man would lay down and die if you gave that gal his truck! Lawd have mercy Jesus!"

"I'll handle Henry," Ruth went on. "I didn't believe the stories about Lazarus either. Had to go see for myself. I was driving one day. I don't know where to, just driving, away from here. Music was blasting in the car, windows rolled down with the wind in my hair. My mind was a million miles away. I was gone..." Ruthie looked far away. Honey Chile and Lilah were quiet.

Just then, Rose left the bathroom and saw the three women in the room, intimate. She hid around the corner to listen.

"Saw him in the middle of the road. At first, I didn't believe it. I had heard, but I didn't *believe*. I thought them stories about Lazarus and them butterflies was crazy, but they was true. They was all true…"

The women stopped and stared at Rose, who had just entered the room.

"What's true?" Rose sounded young, sweet and innocent. Vulnerable.

"That you sleeping with my husband," said Ruthie.

Honey's mouth opened wide and then, slowly, turned into a smile. Her eyes shifted in gleeful anticipation.

"A fight! *A fight!*"

"Hush up, Honey! Ain't nobody fighting in here." Lilah stood in allegiance to Ruthie.

"That's all right, though. I can't give my husband no babies. The least I can do is let him have you." Ruthie all but spat the statement at Rose before she turned on her heels and left. Honey Chile followed like a dog, but not before giving Rose one last potent eye roll.

Finally, Lilah was alone in the room with Rose—there was something about the woman that stirred her. She hated this feeling inside her—she felt she was betraying Ruthie—but there was something in Rose that needed—wanted—to be held, and she was the only one to do it. Lilah saw a slight soft glow around Rose, and then it left as quickly as it came. From her point of view, Rose looked watery, like she was in soft focus.

"Why you sleeping with Henry?" Lilah blurted out.

Rose looked at her. "What's it to you?"

"Ruthie is my friend. She doesn't deserve that."

"And he don't deserve her," Rose said emphatically.

The women looked at each other for a long moment. Lilah squinted and looked at Rose again. Was Rose in the Black Light? Everything was hazy, crazy. Her head was swishing around like water in a bucket from the alcohol. She put her hand to her head and stumbled back.

"You okay?" Rose inched closer to Lilah.

Lilah put her hand up as if to ward her away. "Yes, I'm—" Lilah's arm slumped to the ground. Lights out.

CHAPTER 6

THE LIGHT ON THE CEILING WAS COLD AND WHITE, NOT WARM and dark like the one that held Lilah's Nat. Lilah mumbled and gurgled in her mind and sensed she was in an unfamiliar place. Something about not knowing where she was or how she got there—being lost—gave her an overwhelming sense of peace, and she relaxed into it.

Good, Lilah thought to herself, and she let her head fall deeper into the pillow behind her. Suddenly, the murmurings grew closer, louder. Familiar, like people talking. She was here and not with the Black Light and the reality of it made her head hurt.

"Look! She's opening her eyes!" someone said. Lilah waited. When there was silence, she realized that the murmurings—the people—must have been talking about her. There were people there with her, wherever she was—wherever that was. So she gave them what they wanted and opened her veiled lids with a flutter of her eyes.

"She lives!" It was Honey, making a commotion with her hands, face and body. Lilah marveled at Honey's excitement. She was so expressive.

"Stand back, Honey." The voice was sweet and soothing. Ah, yes. Ruthie. She advanced closer to Lilah, like Rose had done the last time Lilah's eyes were open. "You blacked out at the fish fry, honey. You feeling okay?" It was an odd question. It was tough for Lilah to tell what anything felt like without the alcohol. Because with the alcohol, there was no feeling...

"I need some water." Lilah's throat was as parched as the Sahara. Ruthie poured her a glass and held the cup for her. Nobody knew it, but Ruthie's liquid wasn't the "water" Lilah was referring to, but she sipped, resigned.

"You okay, Lilah?" Ruthie asked again. Lilah wasn't sure, but she knew there was little she hated more than seeing Ruthie look like that. A look of concern and worry. That woman had so much on her already. She'd been such a good and supportive friend. "Samuel went to get your things. He'll be back."

"I'm fine, Ruthie. Really, I am." Lilah managed a weak smile.

Honey pinched Lilah's cheeks so hard they turned red. "See, there's our Lilah! She's alive! Alive and well!" Honey Chile all but screamed. *Not by choice,* said the spirits. *Be careful what you wish for. You just might get it.* Lilah perked up. The voice of the spirits was different from the humans. She heard them first soon after Nat died, but lately, they were getting closer and growing louder. She could only hear them in one ear, though, the left one.

"Y'all go home, now. I'll be fine. Want to get some rest anyway." Lilah managed another smile for Ruthie's sake.

"If I get home now, I can get some dew right before dusk. Mix that with a teaspoon of cow dung and some beer, tomorrow you'll be good as new." Ruthie consoled her, wanting to make it better.

"Promise?" Lilah indulged her friend.

"You know Ruthie always keeps her promises." Ruth touched Lilah's arm—it was ice cold. Ruthie pulled the covers up, tucked Lilah in tight. "I'll be back first thing, you hear?"

"Okay now," Lilah said. Ruthie left, and Honey Chile and her ever-moving arms followed.

Lilah lay there looking at the ceiling. The pain and surprise of still being alive was just too much to bear. It was not want she wanted. Lilah felt like someone put two sticks in her eyelids to keep her eyes open forever, against her wishes.

That's what it feels like when you die, Lilah thought.

She remembered when she saw Nat dead. A cloudy white tear fell from her eyes as she looked around the hospital room. There was a dingy bedpan by the bed. Tubes hung from the walls and from inside machines, beeping, whizzing, and whirring all about her. She looked to the side and saw an old woman sleeping (peacefully?) with an oxygen mask over her face. Lilah envied that woman. "She's on her way. Won't be long now. Tell Nat I'm coming! Big sister's coming!" She trembled and started to get up, to get up to get to where the woman was going.

"Doctor said you supposed to stay put." It was Rose, who sashayed in.

"What you doing here?"

"You fell out when you was talking to me at the fry, remember?" Rose said.

Oh yeah. Right. It was all coming back to Lilah now. She rubbed her head.

"You want some water?" Rose had a cup at the ready.

"Yes! No—well, not the kind you think." Lilah thought about it a moment, then asked: "Why in the hell is somebody always asking me if I want water?"

"'Cause—well, I don't know. Suppose that's what you do when people are sick, I reckon," said Rose.

"I ain't sick."

"Well, something's wrong with you."

"Ain't nothin' 'wrong' with me! Maybe something is 'right,' finally! Maybe something is *right!*" She looked at Rose—there was that soft focus again. Rose had a look of pure caring in her eyes that was undeniable. Lilah saw it and felt hot with shame.

"Besides, I don't like you nohow. Ruthie is in a lot of pain over you sleeping with her husband."

Rose sighed, shook her head. "No woman should be hurt over a man laying with another woman. If she want to be hurt—real hurt—I can think of a list of things longer than my arm she should spend her time on." Rose made the statement so matter-of-factly it hurt.

Lilah looked at her.

"Oh yeah? Like what?" Rose seemed so sure and Lilah wanted to know her thoughts.

"Like not having no money to give your kids on Christmas. Like being accused of something you didn't do. Like having your firstborn son shot and killed by cops. All these things should cause a woman to hurt, hurt real bad. A woman should never take a man sleeping with another woman to heart 'cause it ain't got nothing bad to do with her. That's just a man, chile. He like a bear. His reason for being is all in that thing he got swinging between his legs. When a woman knows that, she knows peace. I wish I could give a seminar, save y'all a lot of pain. I wouldn't even charge—hell, I'd give it to ya for free! The best things in life *are* free, dammit, who says they ain't?"

"You got it all figured out, don't you?" Lilah asked.

"Pretty much sister, pretty much."

"Ain't you ever loved a man before? Ain't you never felt no pain from it?" Lilah probed. There was an untruth in Rose's eyes and she wanted to know more about it—an untold story. She watched the light cast a shadow over Rose's face.

"Love is something you want to keep out of the equation, sugar. It'll be the death of you if you don't." Rose's voice was on the verge.

"How do you go through this life without loving somebody, then?" Lilah asked. She was sincere in her questioning, wanting to know the answer to this very important question.

"Very, very carefully." Rose looked away.

Lilah took her in. "Why you acting so tough?"

"I ain't acting."

"Yes you are. You soft as Red Cross cotton."

Rose laughed out loud and covered her mouth. "Ain't nothing about me soft, nor ever has been. I'm hard as steel, tough as nails."

"Says who?"

"Says my mama! She been telling me that ever since I was five years old! That I ain't got no feeling in me."

"Everybody got feeling in them. If you didn't have no feeling in you, then you'd be dead." Lilah heard herself and burst into tears. Something caught hold inside Lilah, and she began to thrust herself from side to side on the bed.

Rose looked at the girl, shocked. What to do? Finally, she grabbed a box of tissue from the dresser and offered it to her.

"Take it. Take it!" The violent rage was so strong and deep that a single box of tissue hardly seemed like an appropriate cure. But it was all Rose had at the moment, so she offered it. Lilah slowed her thrashing to a stop.

"You crying about your brother?" Lilah was silent. "I heard about Miss Crenshaw hitting him on the side of the road. I heard he was real sweet," Rose offered.

"He was sweeter than sweet! He was the sweetest!" Lilah wailed, striking herself.

"Hey! What you doing?"

"Let me be! Let me be! *Let me be!*" Lilah began hitting herself again, this time without restraint. Rose, frazzled, ran to the door and screamed out.

A nurse came in and called for backup. At a moment's notice, a cavalry of doctors, nurses and aides rushed into the room, all in an attempt to tie Lilah down, help her get a hold of herself. Rose stood back while the people did their jobs, but never once did she take her eyes of Lilah, who had by this point turned a deep shade of crimson. Her eyes were so wild that Rose had to look away. The woman really needed somebody—she was suffering.

Finally, Lilah was restrained by the staff. They gave her an injection and, almost immediately, she dozed off with a faraway, medicated look in her eyes. "She didn't need all that," Rose said to herself. They all filed out, leaving her and Lilah in the room alone. Rose sat and watched Lilah until the sun fell to the earth and the full moon rose high in the sky. Toward dawn, she drifted off to sleep.

Finally, morning arrived. Honey Chile entered first. When she saw Rose fast asleep in the chair, she stopped in her tracks. Ruthie entered next, carrying a potion-filled Tupperware container.

"Well, I'll be," Honey Chile said, seeing Rose asleep. Honey gave Rose a kick accidentally-on-purpose, stirring her awake. "Morning, Rose. Oops, I'm sorry!" she lied. Lilah's eyes fluttered open.

"What you doing here?" Ruthie's tone was accusatory toward Rose.

"Fell asleep, I guess. She was having some problems. The doctors came and—" Rose gestured to the restraints. "She didn't have nobody with her, so I stayed."

"I'm with her. She with her. We *all* with her!" Honey just about spit on Rose's shoe.

"You can leave now. We're here. I'm here." Ruthie's tone was a command and it was final.

Honey Chile looked, waited, and crossed her stubby little arms defiantly in front of her bony body. Rose rose, took up her sweater and her purse, and looked at Lilah. Lilah just stared back, no emotion and no defense.

Finally, Rose just turned and left.

CHAPTER 7

SAMUEL OPENED THE DOOR TO THEIR HOME AND LILAH SQUINTED into the dark room. Her dog, Baby Girl, leapt to her feet in the bestest, proudest, strongest and happiest way a ten-year-old dog could. She rushed Lilah, wagging her tail so hard, far and wide, that her entire body followed. Baby Girl smothered her with welcome-home kisses as Lilah bent down and rubbed her all over.

"All right now." Samuel's strong and sturdy voice slowed Baby's stride, but just a little. "I'm gonna go freshen up. Then I want to talk to you, Lilah. Hear?" Samuel's voice was soft but strong. He looked pointedly at his wife, who finally nodded in reply.

Lilah had met Samuel when she worked over at the five and dime—he'd come there every morning to have his coffee before he went to work. Black, one sugar. That's the way he liked his coffee and that's the way Lilah served it up every morning, seven-thirty sharp. Samuel never missed a day of coffee with Lilah. Lilah liked the fact Samuel had a routine—showed he had some discipline. He wasn't like all the guys her age, that was for sure. Guys her age never seemed to talk about anything she was much interested in. They were always concerned about things like money and flexing their arm muscles 'cause that's what they thought it meant to be a man. Mature men like Samuel were more secure in themselves—a bit "been there, done that," sure, but experienced in the ways of the world in a way that made her feel safe. They didn't have anything to prove like those young'uns.

People used to talk about Lilah and Samuel at first—a young, pretty girl spending time with a man who was almost old enough to be her grandpappy! Lilah and Samuel knew they were the talk of the town, but they were enjoying each other's company too much to care. He talked to her about life and love, and she soaked it all in, offering her take on things he didn't know much about, like women. Samuel was a handsome man who walked the earth like he was ordinary. There was something about his humility—coupled with his discipline—that Lilah thought she could learn from and add on to. He asked and they got married one summer five years ago out in the backyard. Lilah found a dress in the attic and picked some dandelions and daisies for her bridal bouquet. Baby Girl was the ring bearer and Nat was the "best person."

Lilah looked around the room: the old lamp, the old dresser, and the old couch. It seemed everything in the room had a thin film of dust on it, from the gingham curtains on the windows to the doilies on either end of the sofa. Lilah walked toward the liquor cabinet, opened a bottle of gin, and poured it down her throat. She licked her lips. Smiling, she thought, *Now that's my kind of water!* She removed the empty flask at her knee and replenished it with what was left of the liquor bottle, then slid it back in the pouch she'd made before Samuel entered.

"Sit down, Lilah." She did, keeping her hand beside the pouch.

"You all right?" He peered in her eyes as he spoke.

"Fine as can be."

"That ain't the answer to my question." He searched again for her eyes as if he were looking for something, something he couldn't seem to find. Lilah looked up at him, almost girl-like. "Is you all right, I say? You ain't been the same since Nat died."

"Don't think you can ever be the same when your brother's dead. Everything changes, Samuel. Nothing stays the same." Lilah offered this in hopes it would stop the probing.

"I want my old Lilah back." Again he studied her. "Where is she? Is she there? Doctor say keep an eye on you. Told him about the spells you been having."

"Spells? What spells you speaking of, Samuel?"

"The spells you have at night! Some mornings, I wake up and this place looks like a hurricane hit it. The spells where I find you under the table or in the barn, shivering like a newborn babe, where you wake and you don't know what the hell is going on." Samuel looked sadly at his young bride. "I love you, Lilah. Do you still love me?"

She looked up at him. "I do." She meant it. She got up, kissed his bald head and stroked it. "I'm a lucky woman to be loved by a man like you. We ain't got time, but we got love."

"I'm old, Lilah—"

"I know, Samuel. I know." They looked at each other a long while.

"Well then. Swadlow's coming for dinner. Make that fried chicken and them neck bones he likes so much, all right Lilah? He'll be happy. He'll be happy and he'll give me that raise!"

But Samuel wasn't much concerned about the raise. Lilah was about to leave him and he knew it, even before she did. Samuel knew lots of things he never talked about with Lilah; she was too fragile to handle most of them, so he kept those things that would cause unrest to himself. Lilah was growing up, out and away from Samuel, and wasn't nothing he could do about it. That's why he started talking about work, about inviting Swadlow over for dinner, to maintain some kind of normalcy, a routine. Figured he would keep her mind on the routine and forget about all the things she had going on in her heart. Hadn't he provided a great life for her? He went to work every day, there was food on the table, and the mortgage was paid. Wasn't she happy?

Samuel knew it took a lot to make a woman happy. He realized that after his wife divorced him. He didn't know what it was she wanted, and she never told him—she just left. Samuel saw the signs in Lilah, but Lilah's aim wasn't to hurt him and he knew it. She was just young and he had always felt a little guilty about taking this pretty young girl off the market to have for himself. She didn't know all she had to offer the world.

That night, two men who worked at the plant came to dinner, Swadlow and Dickerson. Lilah served them her fried chicken, coleslaw and neck bones with dinner rolls. They all ate hungrily.

"Samuel, you know this is the best fried chicken I had in a month of Sundays. And a pretty young wife, too! Ooh! You a lucky man, a lucky man indeed." Swadlow eyed Lilah hungrily. "You can fill my cup to the top. I like my coffee black. Straight!"

Swadlow placed his hand up the back of Lilah's dress
body could see and squeezed her ass real good. An uns
Samuel beamed at his wife. She was fully into the routine and
he was proud of her.

"You say you like it straight, Mr. Swadlow?" Lilah asked,
never once betraying the fact that she was being felt up by her
husband's boss.

"Straight, no chaser. No cream and no sugar."

Swadlow looked up, smiling at Lilah. She proceeded to pour
the coffee in Swadlow's cup. It filled, spilled onto the saucer and
the table and, finally, overflowed into Swadlow's lap.

"Ahhhhh!" The hot coffee burned him to the bone. Lilah
was steady pouring, her face expressionless.

"Lilah! What are you doing!" Samuel rose to help his boss.

"I'm giving Mr. Swadlow what he asked for. You say you had
quite enough, Mr. Swadlow?" Lilah asked innocently. Swadlow
gulped and then glared at Lilah.

"Just like I thought. Excuse me, gentlemen." Lilah pivoted and
took the empty coffeepot back to the kitchen. Then she rushed
into the bedroom, put a pillow over her face and screamed—a
long, primal wail. Baby Girl looked at her, her full-body wag
slowed to a steady side to side.

❧❧

CHAPTER 8

GRACE'S ROOM WAS A LITTLE GIRL'S HEAVEN: PINK AND WHITE with frills all over. A vanity housed a brush and comb where Grace greased her own head and gave her precious scalp one hundred strokes of the brush just before bedtime, just like her Sweet Mama used to show her. See, Rose Ma wasn't Grace's mother, but Rose always said that just because she didn't birth Grace, didn't mean she wasn't hers. Grace was Rose's child!

Rose had a friend named Beth Anne who used to jump double Dutch with her. They were the double Dutch queens of Sullivan County, and Beth Anne was the only girl who ever trusted Rose enough to be her friend. They used to go everywhere, do everything together.

When she was seventeen, Beth Anne started seeing this guy, Wilson, a good-for-nothing hooty-hoo who banged her up and then left her alone. After she had baby Grace, Beth Anne died. The doctor's said Beth Anne had sickle cell and didn't know it. If Beth Anne would have found out she had the disease before she had Grace, maybe they could. . .well, maybe. Rose always thought about the "maybe" when she thought of Beth Anne. Sweet Mama was Beth Anne's auntie who raised Beth Anne when her mama gave her up at age three. She raised Grace for as long as she could until her sugar made her feet swole up so much that she couldn't hardly stand to change the little girl's diaper no more, or take her to school, or fix her food. She couldn't help Grace with her math, not now that Grace was nine years old. It was enough to drive an old woman insane—and it almost did 'til Rosie came and took Grace off her hands, took her and made her her own almost five years ago.

Grace loved Rose, and she knew that Rose needed her loving more than she needed hers. Sometimes children *do* say the oddest things when really they ain't doing and saying odd things at all, they just speaking and acting to the truth that they see, hear and feel, but mostly hear and feel. And Grace was the same way, especially with Rose Ma. Grace could read Rose's moods like the moon, and she always gave her the space she needed—or the crowd she craved.

Grace liked a boy in school named Jimmy Leon. They fought all the time, him pulling her hair, her sticking her tongue out. But it only made him love her more. Grace was rambunctious, headstrong and sure. Jimmy was quiet, played the guitar and talked so low people always asked him, "Speak up, sonny boy. What'd ya say? Stop mumbling!" Jimmy Leon chased her around the school every day, chased her for a kiss, and she ran so hard and so fast that one day she fell and scraped her knee. She didn't tell nobody because she knew they would ask a lot of questions. Especially Rose Ma. Rose Ma did *not* want Grace to be around boys, and she knew it.

Grace couldn't understand why Rose Ma was asking her more and more about boys, always telling her to cover up and get bigger clothes. But Rose Ma did very little to cover herself up, so Grace didn't know why she went to such great lengths to cover *her* up! Grace noticed the way the men looked at Rose Ma, but she couldn't tell if Rose Ma liked it or not. Rose Ma wore the fancy clothes—the sexy clothes—to attract their attention, but why did she act like she didn't care when they looked? Isn't that what she wanted? Grace couldn't figure out this part of Rose Ma.

Rose and Grace sat close in Grace's twin bed and watched *The Wizard of Oz*. It was the end of the movie, where Dorothy clicks her heels three times and says, "There's no place like home, there's no place like home, there's no place like home." Grace and Rose shared a tub of popcorn between them. Grace looked at the screen, bored—they had seen this movie a million times—but every time they watched it, it was like the first time for Rose Ma. Grace didn't like watching the movie as much as she liked to look at Rose Ma watching it. Rose watched Dorothy with the Scarecrow, the Lion, and Glinda the Good Witch.

"Rose Ma," Grace looked pensive.

"Yeah, baby."

"Is it true what they say about you?"

Rose laughed. "They say a lot of things about your Rose Ma, baby. Don't believe everything you hear."

"Is it true what they say you do behind the red door?"

Rose Ma turned and looked at Grace. "What you say?" Rose was still.

"That you let babies out behind the red door. Is it true?" Grace asked.

Rose Ma turned to look at a smiling Dorothy in her glittery red shoes. "I give a woman a choice if she wants to have a baby or not. It's her body. Don't you think she got a say in what to do with it?" Rose asked, matter-of-fact.

Grace thought about it a moment and shrugged. She didn't know why other people made such a big deal about it when Rose Ma just talked about it so simple like that. It made her feel comfortable to talk about it too. "I guess so."

"Look at me, Grace." Rose held Grace's arms on either side and squeezed them tight when she talked. "I want you to know you always have a choice. Even when you think you don't and your back is to the wall, you got a choice, every minute of every day. Promise me you won't ever forget what your Rose Ma tell you, you hear?" Rose squeezed Grace a bit too tight. The little girl flinched, then searched her eyes.

"Why? You going somewhere?" Grace asked.

"What makes you say that?" Rose kept her eyes glued to Dorothy and the Scarecrow on the screen.

"I'm just saying. If you leave—if you have to leave—please don't send me to be with my daddy. His new wife is fat, and she squeezes me like a lemon!"

"Grace!"

"It's true, Rose Ma! I'm just saying! If you have to go—if you really have to go—will you promise to come back for me?"

Rose looked at Grace and smiled.

"Time for you to get to bed." Rose looked at the TV screen as the credits scrolled to the end. She clicked off the television and walked toward the door.

"Night, Rose Ma."

"Night, Grace."

Rose went to her bedroom and took off her clothes by the light of the moon. Naked, she slid beneath the covers, and just before she turned the lamp out, she opened the drawer in her nightstand and pulled out a picture of herself with a handsome gentleman in happier times. She grimaced as the ever-present pain in her back gripped her long and deep. She touched the photo gently—Solomon—and let the tears fall where they may.

CHAPTER 9

LILAH DRESSED FOR WORK IN THE RED, BLUE, YELLOW AND green outfit that was the uniform of Hot-Dog-on-a-Stick. They had opened up shop in Lucasville a year ago. According to their survey, Southerners were their most loyal customers, so an innovative marketing expert from New York City had the great idea of putting one in every other small town south of the Mason-Dixon Line. Their graphs and charts—filled with suspicious-sounding words and confusing numbers—all indicated that the venture would be a smash hit and bring back its earlier fame of being America's favorite food—the hot dog!

Lilah arrived at Hot-Dog-on-a-Stick at ten o'clock in the morning, her stringy blond hair peeking through the big poufy hat with the tiny brim. Mr. Barnes was a fat and jolly sort. Lilah wondered why he was so happy when his store was doing so poorly, but she liked his enthusiasm. She wanted it all to work out for him—really, she did—but she didn't have the heart to tell him how little the people of Lucasville cared about his fried hot dogs dipped in old, greasy batter. He was a nice man,

Mr. Barnes, and gave her a whole week off with pay when Nat died a year ago so that she could bury her brother. Acts of kindness during times of need were the little things people never forgot, and so Lilah soldiered on for Mr. Barnes's sake, for the sake of his joy. She heard his wife left him after he spent their life savings on the store. He said he was happy to be finally free of her because nothing is worse for a man than to be with a woman who doesn't believe in his dreams.

The store was empty, but that didn't stop Mr. Barnes from coming by with his ever-present clipboard and a smile to preach about things like "attitude," "great customer service" and the merits of "personal hygiene and good grooming." Lilah was numb on the outside, but she rallied hard for Mr. Barnes.

"Lilah, did you get the latest manual about hints and tips to make more sales?"

"Yes sir. Yes sir, I did." She smiled weakly.

"Okay, now we're going to do a little play-acting." Mr. Barnes changed his face so that he could get "in character," acting like a disgruntled customer.

"Good morning! May I take your order?" Lilah asked, fake-cheerily.

"It ain't a good morning." He stuffed his hands in his pockets. Mr. Barnes was really a horrible actor.

"I'm sorry, sir. What's wrong?" Lilah asked. Just then, Mr. Barnes stopped dead in his tracks.

"Lilah, that's not the way you should answer. If a customer is being negative, don't sink down to his level and get into an emotional conversation with him. This is a *business!* You want to make the sale!"

"Yessir, Mr. Barnes—"

"Okay then. Let's go again." Mr. Barnes put on the "disgruntled customer" look again.

"Good morning, sir! May I take your order?" Lilah asked in exactly the same rehearsed and contrived intonation as before.

"Ain't nothing good about this morning," Mr. Barnes repeated. He looked up at Lilah expectantly.

"Well, a hot dog on a stick is sure to make any man's cloud turn into a sun!"

Mr. Barnes snapped out of character and brightened. "That's good, Lilah! That's great!"

"Thank you, Mr. Barnes!" She was happy to have pleased him. Lilah was happy to have pleased anyone—she felt she had done so little of it lately.

"Okay then. Let's continue." Mr. Barnes put on his sad face again. He looked at the menu and squinted. "I'll have a hot dog on a stick and lemonade," Barnes said.

Lilah punched some keys on the register, ringing up the sale. "That'll be five dollars and twenty-five cents, sir."

Mr. Barnes snapped out of character again. "No Lilah, you got to learn to build a sale! When a customer asks for two things, you got to sell them two more! Say, 'Do you want to have a salad to start or a dessert to end?' You know what I'm talking about, don't you Lilah?" Mr. Barnes pleaded with her. He seemed so small and desperate. Lilah just wanted to help him.

"Yes sir. Yes, I do. But, uh…" She looked down.

"What is it, Lilah?"

"Well, we only sell two things, sir: hot dogs and lemonade. I don't have much to work with."

Mr. Barnes considered this. He scratched his head and took some notes. "That's a good point, Lilah. A real good point."

"Maybe I can ask them if they want...two hot dogs and, if they ordered a small, offer them a medium or a large lemonade?"

"Hot diggity dog, Lilah, you got it! You're catching on! That's a great idea!" Mr. Barnes smiled. "You're doing great, just great." Barnes seemed a little too excited over something that Lilah seemed to think was so small and carried so little weight.

Just then, Sally Sue walked in—another employee. Folks around town said Sally Sue and Mr. Barnes were together, and that Sally Sue wanted to help Mr. Barnes succeed so that she could build a secure future for herself. Sally Sue had a little boy named Nicholas who was slow and life was hard for her. She needed someone like Mr. Barnes to give her wealth and joy—but this hot dog thing had to succeed. She worried about Lilah, who was a little too blond, a little too young, and whose tits were just a little too perky. Sally Sue looked at Lilah, then smiled over Mr. Barnes's way.

"Mr. Barnes." (Nobody knew why she called him Mr. Barnes. Everybody knew she was sleeping in his bed and wanted more.) "Mr. Barnes," she said anyway, "can I speak with you a moment? It's important."

"Why yes, Sally Sue! But of course!" Mr. Barnes scooped up his clipboard and looked at Lilah. "Will you be able to hold down the fort without me?" Mr. Barnes asked.

"Oh! Well, uh, yes! I'll think I'll be able to manage."

"Good, Lilah. Very good." He smiled and went with Sally Sue, who looked back and gave Lilah the evil eye.

Lilah didn't see Miss Crenshaw come in, she just noticed that she seemed to appear—right in front of her—without notice or warning. Miss Crenshaw looked up and seemed startled to find Lilah there with her sunny hat and top and her sad, red-rimmed eyes. Miss Crenshaw felt the pang of guilt in her gut, but she carried on with no identifiable sign of remorse or sympathy.

"I'll have a hot dog on a stick and small lemonade, please." Miss Crenshaw avoided Lilah's gaze.

"Would you like to make your small into a medium?" Lilah looked at her, the woman who killed her brother. She felt bewildered.

"No. Why would I want to do that?" Miss Crenshaw shook her head in a condescending way.

"Just asking. Just doing my job."

"Well, you'd do a better job by getting me just what I asked for. The hot dog and the lemonade, please." Miss Crenshaw had her five-dollar bill clenched in her tight and bony hand like she didn't want to ever let it go. Miss Crenshaw knew the value of things even when most people didn't. Didn't matter if she was a wealthy woman—a dollar is a dollar and a million is a million, hell! There was nothing that Miss Crenshaw hated more than waste.

Lilah slowly spiraled down into her hazy state where she could see the Black Light. She turned by rote and bagged the hot dog. Next, she filled a small cup with ice and poured some lemonade into it. Finally, she put a lid on top, checked it twice for fit, and handed Miss Crenshaw her bag with the hot dog and the lemonade inside.

"That'll be five twenty-five, ma'am."

"Five twenty-five! What happened? Your prices went up!"

"No ma'am. It's been five twenty-five since we opened for a hot dog and a lemonade. Prices never changed, stayed the same."

Miss Crenshaw sucked her teeth. Never once in the whole exchange did she make eye contact with Lilah, and Lilah never once took her eyes off her. She observed Miss Crenshaw's liver-spotted, crepe paper skin and the oddly stiff hat that perched on her head. She seemed always to be overdressed for the occasion—certainly overdressed for an excursion to buy a hot dog and lemonade—but it was probably due to the way folks in Miss Crenshaw's generation did things. Their image and what society might think of them were important. Lilah looked at the woman in awe; Miss Crenshaw was the last one to see Nat alive before she hit him with her car and killed him.

"...ten, eleven..." Miss Crenshaw was busy counting her pennies to get to twenty-five cents, so this would take some time. Lilah used all this time to drink this woman in in a way she had never done before with another live human being. *She was the last person to see Nat alive*, she thought again, and in that, Miss Crenshaw was special—sacred.

"...twenty, twenty-one." The counting was almost over now. In those final moments, Lilah thought about what Miss Crenshaw would do with all her unspent money she wasted. She had one foot in the grave and could never take it with her.

Lilah stuck her hand out to receive the change. Miss Crenshaw looked at her outstretched hand for a long time. Would she place it in Lilah's hand or would she put it on the counter? Lilah watched her as she grappled with the moment, but she stayed firm, steady.

Miss Crenshaw put her penny-filled hand toward the counter and looked up at Lilah. Miss Crenshaw saw that the girl was longing for a connection to her brother that only she—the one who killed him—could give her, and probably, maybe, if she gave this girl the money in her hand, the nightmares of what she'd done to this boy would cease and she could get some sleep at night. Yes. She would do it. She decided that she would give the small change to Lilah in her hand, and so she did. Their hands grazed—touched—just a moment in the exchange, but that was enough. It was enough for the both of them.

"There, that's it." Miss Crenshaw looked at Lilah a moment, then took her hand away.

"Thank you, ma'am. Have a nice day."

CHAPTER 10

Honey Chile lay in bed, waiting. Pop-Pop came out of the bathroom, clean as a whistle and smiling at his wife.

"Baby? I'm gonna get me some honey tonight! You ready for papa bear to tear dat ass up?"

"Oh yeah. I'm ready all right. You eat all your dinner today, baby?"

"You know I did! Every spoonful." Pop-Pop licked his lips and roared like a lion. He was horny, but his eyes fluttered. He had no idea why.

"Good. That's real good." Pop-Pop got in bed under the covers with his wife and turned off the light. Honey didn't move a muscle. Pop-Pop used his hands to explore his wife's womanly parts, roughly, like sandpaper. Honey Chile winced and stiffened, but didn't say a word. Pop-Pop nuzzled her neck. He yawned loudly, and she smiled. Pop-Pop started toward her breasts and yawned again—this time longer and with more gusto. Finally, the petting slowed to a halt, then to a dead stop. Honey smiled wider and relaxed.

Pop-Pop rolled over on the other side of the bed. "I'm sorry, babe. I'm just too tired tonight. Can you forgive Pop-Pop?"

"Don't worry about it, baby. Don't worry." Honey Chile watched her husband snuggle into his pillow and close his eyes.

"Night, baby."

"Night." Honey Chile looked up at the ceiling and finally, slowly, closed her eyes. Ruthie's potion worked! The sweet taste of success.

CHAPTER 11

ROSE SAT ON THE PORCH AND WAITED FOR THE GIRL TO ARRIVE. While she waited, she smoked a cigarette to calm herself. Finally, she saw the girl walking up the dirt road and she almost gagged. Etta Mae was so young. Rose had known her all her life—ever since she was in her mama's belly—and now, here she was, carrying a child of her own and coming to Rose for the remedy. Etta Mae came closer, and Rose could see the full view of her now. She looked at the young girl's belly, which was still flat. It was early, but there was no more time. Rose knew it and Etta Mae knew it too.

Finally, she arrived at the porch and looked at Rose. Rose looked at her carefully, waiting for her to confirm. The girl was silent. Then she strode past Rose on the porch and entered through the red door, the red door with the butter-flies on it—and left it open just a little bit for Rose to come inside. Rose threw her cigarette on the ground, squashed the burning ash and followed the girl into the red room. When Etta Mae left an hour later, Rose went into the bathroom and threw up.

"I can't do this no more," Rose said to herself.

CHAPTER 12

SAMUEL LAY IN BED AND STROKED HIS YOUNG WIFE'S HEAD. HE was old, he was dying, and he knew it. Some illness would befall him soon, or maybe not, maybe he would just die of old age, but he knew the end was near. If Lilah stayed, she would do everything she could to join him because she had no reason for being anymore without him, now that Nat was gone. They'd agreed long ago that if she wanted out of their marriage he would give it to her, but he had a better idea.

Lilah awoke to clanging pots in the kitchen. She looked at the time: it was seven thirty. She was relieved to find that she was not under the table or bunched in the attic, that she was in bed, safe and sound, with Baby Girl curled at her feet. Baby Girl looked wide-eyed this morning; that was the first indication that there was something different. Something had changed, simply because it had to. She got herself out of bed, reached for the flask in the drawer of the bedside table and took a swig. The drink hit her strong this time of morning, stinging her eyes and making them water.

Again there was clanking in the kitchen and then a yelp.

"Dang it!" Lilah rushed out in her robe while Baby Girl followed, all the while knowing. When Lilah entered the kitchen, she saw Samuel at the stove with the flame too high and white smoke coming from a pan on the stove.

"Samuel! What are you doing?" She turned off the burner and looked at the burnt eggs. The burnt toast had already found its home on a blue-patterned plate. There was juice and coffee, too.

"The meat didn't turn out too good." He showed her four strips of bacon that looked like leather.

"What you doing this for, Samuel?"

"I'm doing it for you." Samuel looked at her lovingly.

"Making me breakfast? Why? You know I always make you breakfast in the morning, Samuel. Why you doing that?"

"Something's changed, Lilah." Finally, she noticed the funny look in his eyes that told her to stop what she was doing and sit. So she did. And waited.

"It's time for you to go. I know we agreed a long time ago that I would turn you loose if you wanted to. I'm afraid if you don't go now, you'll find a reason to stay and you'll die."

"Samuel! What you saying?"

"You got too much life to live to spend it in Lucasville. This is a place for me to die, not you. It's time to leave, Lilah." He pointed to the door.

"I've packed your bags for you. Didn't know what you liked, so I did the best I could and chose the things I saw you wear the most. You got fresh, clean underwear—bra and panties, the frilly ones you like with the days of the week, not the uncomfortable ones I know you only wore for me. I bought a big bag of food for Baby Girl, so you'll have some to get to wherever you're going. Here's everything I got." He handed her a wad of cash. "That should keep you for a good long while." He looked at her, blinking.

"Samuel? You all right?"

"Better than ever, Lilah. And you're going to be, too. You're going to be all right."

"I'm not leaving you here by yourself! I don't want to go nowhere—"

"Yes, but you need to."

"Samuel! Are you kicking me out of my house now?"

"Yes. You got to be gone by the time I get back from work. I got to go bathe now. Get ready." He rose, walked toward the back where the bedroom was. Quiet as a mouse.

"Samuel," she whispered. She couldn't make any sense of it, but somewhere deep inside, she knew he was right. She couldn't figure out *why* he was, just *that* he was. She looked at the wad of money in her hands and fingered it gently. Baby Girl looked up at her with consoling eyes and something that faintly resembled a smile. She must have sat there for a while because, when she looked up, Samuel was there again, dressed and ready for work. She stood up to meet his eyes, and he took her tiny head in his hands.

"You got something you ain't using. Find out what it is and use it, use it till you can't use it no more. That will see you through." He smiled warmly and moved the piece of hair that was obstructing Lilah's left blue eye. "Fly, butterfly." He kissed her slowly, sweetly on the lips, patted Baby Girl's head and walked out the door. Lilah ran to the window to watch him leave, watch him walk away from her.

After he left, she noticed Rose sitting across the street under the magnolia tree. Her hand was on the tree, as if she were holding it up. Lilah watched her a long while, wondering what she was doing there and why. Finally, she walked outside. Baby tried to follow, but she wouldn't let her. "Not now, Baby. Mama got something to do and she doesn't need your nose in it." As if she could hear and understand, Baby Girl put her tail between her legs, bent her ears back and back-tracked into the house. Lilah closed the door slowly behind her.

In her housecoat and slippers, Lilah crossed the road and got a better look at Rose.

"What you doing?"

"Nothing much." Rose stayed still.

"Well, thank you for staying up with me in the hospital. That was real nice of you." Rose just shrugged her shoulders and cast her eyes up the road, like she was looking for something.

"Looking for something?"

"Yeah, someplace to be, somewhere to go. Can't stand it here no more. 'Bout to jump out of my skin." Rose let this revelation out like a shriek.

Lilah smiled and asked: "Where you wanna go?"

Rose thought a good long while. She sucked a deep breath, as if she had been waiting for someone to ask her this for a long time. "Newhope." Then, she exhaled; finally someone had given her permission to let go. "I want to go to Newhope."

Lilah nodded. "Well then, Newhope it is."

CHAPTER 13

"THAT SAMUEL. FULL OF SURPRISES." RUTHIE LAUGHED. SHE looked at her young friend. "So? You gonna go?"

"Guess so. Samuel say he want me gone by nightfall," Lilah explained.

Ruthie laughed. "That man got a heart of gold. Always had."

"I'm gonna miss him." Lilah looked away. "Guess who's going with me?"

Rose paced at the door. Grace entered like clockwork, three fifteen, straight from school. Her dress and knobby knees were a fright from a hard day of running away from Jimmy Leon's kisses.

"Hey, Rose Ma!" She entered hastily, like she was rushing to get somewhere new.

"Hey, young missy! Don't Rose Ma get a kiss?" Grace stopped herself in her tracks and slowly turned. She looked incredulously at Rose Ma.

"A kiss? My Rose Ma wants a kiss?"

"As a matter of fact I do. Something wrong with that?" Grace beamed. She ran to Rose Ma, threw her tiny arms around her neck, and showered the woman's face with kisses. Rose couldn't help but laugh, and she received them all eagerly. She hugged the little girl tight. During the embrace, Grace noticed the packed bags at the door.

"Going somewhere?" Grace asked, but she knew.

"I'm gonna come back for you, Grace." The statement was more a question, like she was asking for permission. Grace touched her Rose Ma's face and looked her in the eye.

"How bad you got to go?"

"Bad, baby. Real bad."

Grace considered this a long while. Finally, she accepted it. "Okay."

⟡

Ruthie opened the door to find Rose and Grace on her door step. Rose was shaken.

"What you want around here, Rose? Ain't you got enough?" Ruth asked, accusatory.

"I want you to take Grace." Rose was shaky when she said this. Ruthie took her in—she had never seen Rose in such a state. Ruthie looked down at the smiling little girl. So grown, Gracie was. She'd always wanted a little girl just like her.

"I know you'll see that she gets what she needs. Lilah and me, we taking a little trip to Newhope."

Ruthie looked at her. Her eyes went quiet inside.

"He's married now, Rose. But that don't seem to matter to a woman like you, do it?"

Rose, however, didn't skip a beat. "Like I said, Lilah and I are taking a little trip, and Grace is gonna need a woman to look after her while I'm gone. She's getting to be that age now." Grace shifted, blinked and waited. Ruthie looked down at her.

"What do you think about that?" Ruthie's question was pointed to the little girl. Grace rolled this over in her mind.

"Can we cook cornbread every day?" Grace asked.

"Cook cornbread on Fridays. Only on Fridays." That was the end of the negotiation.

Grace weighed her options. Finally, she settled.

"Friday's good with me." Grace spontaneously reached for Ruthie's neck and hugged it. The simple gesture overwhelmed her. Ruthie fought hard to stifle a tear.

"Why don't you go in the spare room and get yourself settled? We can pick up your things in the morning."

"Yes ma'am." The little one was a sassy girl, but she was a good girl. She turned to Rose. "Bye, Rose Ma. When you coming back?"

Rose considered the question. She kept her answer honest, simple, and true. That had been the hallmark of their relationship—why would she stop now? "When I do." And that was that. Rose bent to hug the little girl. "I want you to be a good girl for Miss Ruthie, you hear?"

"Yes ma'am."

"I hear you sassing anybody, I'm liable to pick up where I'm at and correct that tail of yours. You got that?"

"Get it. Got it."

"Good."

Grace made her way into the house like she owned it, found her room and settled. Rose and Ruthie stood face to face at the door.

"Thought Grace would be good for you. Good for you and Henry." It was Rose's way of asking and thanking at the same time.

"How thoughtful of you." Ruthie's words were filled with venom, but there was a tinge of something heartfelt beneath the words. Ruthie snatched the keys off a nail in the wall.

"Be sure to watch the gas gauge. It don't always mean what it say." With that, Ruth slammed the door in Rose's face. Rose registered a moment of guilt, and then she smiled, proud of herself.

Rose came barreling out with her bags. Lilah jumped out of Henry's truck and lifted the big old bag filled with food for Baby Girl to make room for Rose's things. Baby Girl, tail wagging behind her, perked up when she saw Rose.

"Who's this?"

"That's Baby!" With this, Baby Girl jumped up on Rose in blissful, full-body-wag mode.

"I'm allergic to dogs! I hate them!"

"You're allergic?"

"Yes! I'm allergic! That dog can't go!" Rose looked down at the enthusiastic dog. Baby Girl was ready to travel!

"But I can't leave her!"

"Why not?"

"Baby's sick! She ain't got that long to live!"

"Jesus. Jesus! This ain't gonna work for me!" Rose started to take her things out of the back of the truck.

"Hey! Where you going?" wailed Lilah. "Rose!"

Rose turned.

"You didn't tell me we was gonna drive fifteen hundred miles with no sick goddamned dog!"

"I told you I had to bring my Baby!"

"I thought you meant baby as in wah, wah *baby!*" Rose mock-cried like an infant. Lilah laughed at the brutal imitation.

"Look, Baby can help us along the way. She's a good watch-dog! She'll keep us safe. We need her." Baby Girl started barking excitedly, as if she knew she was being talked about and liked it. "She'll stay in the back. I promise, she ain't gonna be no trouble to you. No trouble to you at all. I can't—"

Lilah took a deep breath. Pleading now, it was all she could muster to say the rest of it. "My brother gave me Baby. I can't leave her." There it was. The declaration came out like a sigh. Rose saw the effort it took for Lilah to talk about this, about Nat, and her heart overflowed with compassion for her. The two women were silent a long while, considering. Finally, Rose picked up her bags, turned back toward the truck and threw her stuff in the back. Lilah and Baby yelped with joy.

"Yippee! Newhope, here we come!"

CHAPTER 14

HENRY WOKE UP BEFORE RUTHIE. HE HADN'T SEEN ROSE IN a few days, and he was going through withdrawal. Called her a couple of times, but got no response. He was forlorn. He was in love and he felt like a fool to think a woman like her could ever be in love with a man like him. He was lucky to have her as long as he did. *Hell, all we have is every day, and we ain't even promised that,* he thought. *At least I can say I tasted heaven's pie.*

He slipped on his pants and shirt from yesterday, careful not to wake up Ruthie, who seemed to be sleeping real sound these days, almost like she was relieved of something. He knew she probably knew about his relationship with Rose. He never wanted to hurt his wife. He loved Ruthie! Ever since high school, she had been his heart, but somehow—and he didn't even understand it himself—there seemed to be another part of his heart that had belonged totally and fully to Rose, a part he never even knew existed. His feelings for Rose were strong—probably the most powerful ones he'd ever had in his life. It was more than just sex. Rose was just so free. He wondered if she cared about anything,

anything at all—she was just so comfortable with herself, in her body, inside her skin. Rose's freedom was a rare and wonderful thing, and he thought he could capture some part of it when he went deep inside of her, that he could touch the source of all creation and creativity.

He walked outside. It was so early in the morning, it was still dark. He walked down the steps of his porch, lost deep in the thought of Rose and the flower at the center of herself. He stopped where he left it last—before he noticed it was gone. He looked, then looked again. He looked in the street, around the corner—he looked. No tire marks, no evidence, no nothing. Jesus! It was gone!

"Ruthie! Where's my truck?"

Ruthie lay in bed, but she was wide awake. She opened her eyes and smiled.

The commotion woke little Grace, who wasn't asleep neither. She lay in bed thinking about her Rose Ma, about where she was going and if she was going to be all right. There was a part of her that felt protective of her Rose Ma—even though she seemed strong, Grace knew she was really soft. Grace felt there weren't a whole lot of people who knew that, but she did. She knew her Rose Ma would miss her—probably more than she would miss her Rose Ma—and the thought gave her a pain inside. She breathed into it and said a tiny prayer, then she closed her eyes and fell back asleep, storing her strength to ward off Jimmy and his kisses in the morning.

୧୨

CATERPILLAR

the wormlike larva of a butterfly or moth

CHAPTER 15

LAZARUS LAY IN WAIT FOR THE GIRLS' ARRIVAL. THE SPIRITS HAD "telephoned" him in his left ear and described what they looked like. Lazarus wasn't the type of man who based anything on what he saw, but what he felt, and he knew that he'd know precisely when the girls arrived. In the meantime, there was much to be done in the garden to summon the butterflies in celebration of their arrival.

Lazarus was an odd man to the folks in Newhope. He measured six feet five inches had blue-black skin and always wore a pair of denim overalls. He wore his hair long in twisty dreadlocks and the whites of his eyes were white-white. He didn't talk much—some said they never heard Lazarus utter a word—just every now and again he'd offer a grunt, affirmative or no. When people talked to him, they thought to themselves that he seemed to be a man who was always listening between the words. They didn't know how to take him, so they said little to him and he said even less to them. Lazarus felt that talking was overrated and folks just did too much of it. It was words that got people into trouble, words that waged wars and killed women and children. People used words with such reckless abandon that he used them hardly if ever at all, and he liked it that way. That was his contribution—being silent—his way of countering the hurtful things he had seen people do to themselves and each other.

He sold the vegetables he grew in his garden: tomatoes, collards, butter beans, squash and kale. People came from miles around to buy the things Lazarus grew in his garden. There was a chef from a fancy restaurant in New York who even had Lazarus's vegetables flown in! Lazarus must have made a lot of money from this alone, but he always found time to give away some fresh vegetables to the folks in town he knew didn't have enough to eat. Every Friday, you'd see Lazarus walking down the road with his butterflies and his dogs, leaving a brown paper bag full of vegetables on the stoops of those he knew were hungry. He always kept his door unlocked, but nobody ever went in.

Lazarus wanted for nothing. He ate very little himself, drank some, mostly water. He had long bouts of sleep, as that was the way he could get in touch with his dreams—which were, in fact, the dreams of others. He lay in wait for them at night, the spirits who would communicate to Lazarus the folks who needed his help after having just let go of something. There is a natural instability when a person has just interfaced with the darkest part of his or her soul. Lazarus thought of himself as the bridge from the place they left to their future, where the footing was strong and sure. Some lucky folks (though they didn't know how lucky they were) were chosen by the spirits because they had done the work, the hard work of committing to change their lives for something better, wider, and deeper. The spirits always wished they had more work to do, more people who let go, more folks to send to Lazarus, more people who wanted to change, but the spirits knew that the ones who did were always sufficient.

The girls drove quite a ways before they embarked on an open stretch of road where they didn't have other cars in front of them. Baby Girl was coiled up like a ball in the back of the truck with a half-spilled bowl of fresh water. She was content. Lilah looked back at her and rubbed her soft black ears. Baby Girl was old. Lilah had to put three drops of medicine in her food several times a day just to keep Baby here on earth, and she wondered if she was doing the right thing. Maybe it would be best to let Baby slip away into the darkness—or into the light, like Nat—but she needed Baby here. Was she being selfish? If she was, she hadn't meant to be. She just needed so much right now.

Baby's coat was soft as cashmere. She was a sprightly sort when she was young—playful and full of boundless energy. There wasn't nothing Baby wouldn't do for a yellow tennis ball. If you sat anywhere near her collection of well-chewed-on balls, she would pick one up with her mouth and bring it to you— even put it in your hands—to make it easier for you to throw and to play with her. She still had the spirit for this. She could do this all day, every day, nonstop. And every time you threw it, it would be like it was the first time. If Lilah learned anything from Baby Girl—every pet keeper has a ton to learn from their animals—she learned to play, for Lilah was playful by her very nature, but the recent course of events in her life seemed to quench her lightheartedness.

Lilah remembered a time she was going to be in a play at school called *The Little Birch Tree*. The day she was cast, she was so happy she ran all the way home from school. True, the role of the birch tree didn't have anything to do but stand on stage and listen and watch others sing, dance, and talk around it and about it, but it was the center of attention, which both filled her with awe and scared her.

After she got the part, there was whispering in class about how she thought she was better than them now. Fat Doreen wanted to fight her after school at three o'clock because she said she thought she was cute. The truth was, Lilah never thought she was cute a day in her life. She thought she was nice, but never cute, and she wondered why fat Doreen wanted to fight her in the first place. For days, Lilah begged and pleaded with her mother not to be sent to school, saying she had a stomachache or some other incurable sickness. Bernice was determined that Lilah was not going to end up like her—always taking the easy way out—and insisted her eldest child go to school, no matter what.

Lilah made every attempt to hide from Doreen that day, but finally it turned three o'clock and it seemed there was no escaping the inevitable. The last bell rang and the entire school poured out the front door in anticipation of the fight between Doreen and Lilah. The kids all but carried Lilah into the ring and threw her to Doreen, who began pummeling Lilah with her tiny little fists. Doreen was a pro at fighting, and Lilah was not the first frail and happy little girl she'd fought in school for similar offenses like "acting cute," "being smart," and the like. Lilah searched her brain to think what she had done to receive this type of treatment, and all she could think of was that she got cast in *The Little Birch Tree*. She would never give up the part, she knew that for sure, and so she would have to fight. Lilah received Doreen's blows. Somewhere around the sixth or seventh slug, however, something rose up in Lilah and she hauled back and socked Doreen square in the stomach—after that, Lilah took off like a bat out of hell. She ran straight for home, barreling down that hill like her life depended on it, because it did. So Lilah was safe. Baby Girl, all coiled up like a ball in the back of the truck, safe, reminded her of the time in her life when she was safe at home after her near-death at the hands of Doreen.

While they drove, Lilah looked over at Rose. *Guess Ruthie's roots worked after all. Rose is away from Henry now, isn't she?* She smiled at the thought that she had had a hand in rescuing her Ruthie from misery by getting Rose out of town. She never thought she would end up here. Now. With Rose. Not in a million years. Life is funny that way. Lilah reached in the back and took a swig from a flask, then offered it to Rose. Thirsty, Rose put the flask to her mouth and threw her head back. She gagged.

"What the hell is this?"

"It's water!" Lilah beamed.

"This ain't no water."

"Ain't water to you, but it is to me." Lilah snatched her flask back from the ungrateful hussy. Her "water" was far too precious a resource to be rejected by anyone.

"I don't drink," Rose said. Lilah looked at her, incredulous. "Why do people always look at me like that when I say that I don't drink?"

"'Cause you don't seem like the type!"

"The type to not drink? What does this 'type' look like?"

"Glasses, homely. You know." Lilah took a gander at Rose, then took another sip from the flask.

"My daddy died of the stuff. Never put it to my lips until today."

"That's good. Good for you." Lilah was sincere. Alcohol was a hard thing to wean oneself off of, she knew. "Where your people from?" she asked Rose.

"Memphis."

"Ooh, Memphis! The City of Singers! You meet anyone famous?"

"Me and Elvis went way back!"

Lilah looked at her, wide-eyed. "Are you serious? Hot diggity dog! You actually met him? You met the King? Ooh wee!" Lilah was a singer, but she regarded those who made a living at the profession as being outside of herself. Singing was Lilah's dream, but she never talked about it, lest she would be disappointed by putting her time and energy into something that wasn't ever going to come true. It mattered too much as a dream to gamble on in reality. When she saw singers onstage belting out a tune, she couldn't help but stare: it took a certain amount of courage to bypass your fears and pursue the thing that gave you your heart's greatest joy. Also, Lilah was already so childlike, so she always thought that she should choose more serious things to do with her time, like work in an office or become a doctor or a lawyer. But no, she wanted to sing and always had. People told her she was good at it and she thought about pursuing it, but when Samuel asked her to marry him, they made an unspoken agreement that she would never mention the subject again. Now with Samuel letting her go today, she was set free to pursue the real true love of her life.

"You real gullible, you know that?" Rose said to Lilah. "Don't believe everything you hear. How old are you, anyway?"

"Thirty-three. You?"

"Thirty-three. Thirty-three! Girl, you gonna be forty in seven years! Forty years old! What you gonna do about that?"

"Jesus was thirty-three when he died. Nothing I can do but live, I reckon," Lilah said. "And drink, of course." She took another swig from her flask. "Forty probably won't feel the way I think it will. When I was twenty, I used to look at people who were thirty and feel sad for them. They didn't do the things they said they wanted to do—and they sure as hell didn't have the things they said they was gonna have. It's like they got settled with the disappointment, just accepted what life brought them."

Rose nodded her head in agreement. "Yeah, like the fight is gone." Rose thought a moment and then said, "But that don't sound so bad. Wouldn't mind a life without the fight." There was a bend in the road—Rose turned the steering wheel to the left and looked at Lilah. "Good thing you still look twenty-five. Twenty-six at the most."

"Used to hate looking so young when I was a girl. But now..." Lilah raised her flask to the heavens.

"You don't want no kids?" Rose asked.

"Not a matter of wanting them or not wanting them. Just never happened, I guess. Well, just this one time I got pregnant."

"I ain't never had a child myself," said Rose.

"What about Grace?"

"Grace was a gift from a friend who died. I'm Grace's godmother."

"You took her in as your own?" Lilah looked over at Rose.

"Just 'cause I didn't birth her don't mean she ain't mine."

A long moment passed between the women where nothing was spoken. It seemed they were both processing the information given and received, making assessments, surmises, pondering more questions.

"Is it true what they say about you?" Lilah asked.

"Depends on what they say."

"That you let babies out." Rose's silence spoke volumes.

"I'll never forget the day I let that baby out," Lilah said, remembering. "I was nineteen, he was twenty-nine. Married. It was the last time I ever had a man in me and I didn't feel no fear."

"Ain't no need to fear a man in you. Men are just like kids, you know," Rose said knowingly.

"I think you right about that. Don't matter how old they are either, every one of them is still a little boy inside. I can remember the day I figured it out. I felt like a real idiot, giving them so much credit the way I did. Men ain't that bright. They real simple."

"Men want three things: pussy, food, and money."

"In that order?" Lilah asks.

Rose thought for a moment. "Depends on the man I guess." She looked away.

"I'm glad you left Lucasville. Ruthie was beside herself over you sleeping with Henry."

Rose just shook her head, waving it away. "They got Grace between them now. Grace will get them together again."

"I hope you right about that," Lilah said sincerely.

"Grace don't fail, Lilah. Grace never fails." They drove in silence and watched the sun make its way to the other side of the world.

CHAPTER 16

THE GIRLS DROVE ALL DAY WITH VIRTUALLY NO REST AND DAY turned into night again. They switched seats once 'cause Rose was tired of driving, so Lilah took the wheel; she had been driving for almost ten straight hours. Rose dozed, but Baby was wide awake, tail wagging. Lilah reached for her flask but it was empty. Lilah looked over at Rose and thought she wasn't so strong—not as strong as Lilah had thought—and Rose certainly wasn't as tough as people made her out to be. Lilah knew that *she* was stronger—from the inside out—but it wasn't no use telling someone like Rose that, someone whose identity was all tied up into that. Let it be. She looked out at the white lines on the road; they appeared to be zigzagging. Lilah missed Nat terribly while she was driving. She thought she would give the world to see him once more, if only for just a moment. But Nat was in heaven and she was here, in hell. She rubbed her head. The zigzagging lines on the road started to quicken.

"I need to stop." Lilah pulled over violently, put the truck in park and turned off the ignition.

Rose stirred from the abrupt stop. "What'cha doin'?" Lilah grabbed Rose's bag. Rose snatched it back and held it close to her chest. "What'cha doing? That's my bag!"

"I need a tissue!"

"Ain't no tissue in there!" Rose guarded the bag with her life and Lilah wondered what she was keeping in it. She vowed to find out sooner or later, by hook or by crook. Suddenly, Lilah felt violently ill. She ejected herself from the seat and vomited. Rose watched, not fazed in the least.

"You pregnant?"

"Pregnant? That's the worst thing could ever happen right now." Lilah started gagging—there was a bit more bile left in her stomach to come out. "Too much water is all."

"You need something in your stomach. Something to soak up all that 'water.'" Rose reached in the back and pulled out two soggy, sorry homemade fried chicken sandwiches she had prepared just for the trip. Excited by the prospect of food for the road, she had spent time cleaning and flouring the bird the way she had seen her mama do. She fried it real hard so it was crispy on the outside. Only thing is, the last time she fried chicken, it was done on the outside but bloody raw to the bone on the inside. Grace was sick for days because of the raw chicken she fried. Rose wasn't sure if this batch was done any better. She gave it to Lilah, hopeful she would like it. Lilah was her guinea pig.

"How it taste?" Rose asked, hopeful.

Lilah responded by spitting the food to the ground. "Jesus! How much pepper you put in that thing?"

"Just a little." Rose winced. Lilah started to cough and handed the sandwich back to Rose. "Aw, it ain't that bad."

"You say so." Lilah looked around. The road before them looked endless, a glorious proposition for Lilah. "That road is ripe for walking."

"Walking? Where you gonna walk to this time of night?" Rose asked.

"Wherever the road takes me. Walk off some of this water." Lilah stumbled.

"Girl, you don't need to be walking nowhere. You can barely stand up!"

"Walking's the only thing that'll help." Lilah sounded like she had some experience in this department, as if she'd done it a time or two and knew it worked. She set out alone for the open road.

"How long you gonna be?"

"Not long." Lilah started off and Baby Girl stirred to follow. "Stay, Baby. Mama needs a minute." Lilah looked at Rose and Rose looked at Lilah.

"What you think, you gonna leave her here with me? I don't know nothing about no dogs!"

"You don't need to know nothing. Baby Girl will do all the work. She'll protect you, won't you, Baby?" Baby wagged her tail—affirmative. "I'll be right back."

Left alone with Baby, Rose looked down at the dog, whose tongue was halfway out her mouth. She took another bite of her fried chicken sandwich, tried to chew, then spit it out on the ground. Baby went for the food and ate it happily.

"That's it, Baby. You like Rose Ma's cooking, don't you Baby Girl?" Baby ate the soggy sandwich like she'd just hit the jackpot. Dry dog vittles from a bag just gets boring after a while—it's a fact that only a dog could understand and appreciate. She bent down to stroke Baby, grateful her cooking didn't go unappreciated. "That's a good girl." Rose beamed. She sat on the damp earth and wrapped her sweater close around her shoulders.

There was a sudden chill in the air.

It was early morning now, but the sun wasn't too high in the sky. Lilah found a clearing in the road—round the bend was an old, old graveyard. She stopped at a newly minted headstone and squinted, but the name and date on the stone was irrelevant. The person was dead and in the ground, and it was all Lilah needed to feel a bond to her brother. The delusional transference was severe, and it was heightened by her intoxicated state.

"Oh, Nathaniel. How I miss you, baby brother." Lilah wailed a torrent of tears. She sat down on the grave. "Oh, how I wish you could be here with me right now, but you knew. You always knew. This world ain't all it's cracked up to be, Nat. It ain't. You had the right idea, checking out early. Why did you leave me, Nat? If I could have been there, right there when it happened, I would have thrown my body over yours to protect you. Big sister would have been there to protect you, but I couldn't. I didn't. I wasn't. I wasn't!" Lilah struggled to keep her eyes open.

"It ain't been the same, Nat. Not none of it. It's like someone hacked me in two and I ain't been right ever since. I see the world sideways now. But you sent me Baby Girl. If it wasn't for Baby, brother, I don't know. I just don't know..." She held the heart-shaped locket Nat had given to her for her sweet sixteen.

She put it on the day Nat gave it to her and she never took it off. Nat gave her the box and never once did his eyes leave her face when she opened it and let out a shriek of joy that was heard miles away. Nat never thought he would make anyone as happy as he made his sister that day, and it gave him such a sense of joy and accomplishment that he took it with him to his grave. Lilah was just a special sort—misunderstood—but he accepted and loved her.

Lilah placed the necklace on the grave. "I'm gonna give this to you for good luck! Not that you need luck if you're dead, but well, hell. I want you to have it just the same." The glint of the necklace caught a light nearby. Lilah, compelled by the sight of the light dancing seductively before her, started toward it. She squinted and saw a fleeting image of a handsome young man with blond, curly hair: her brother.

"Nat!"

She opened her eyes wide and blinked. It was Nat alright, in the same jeans and plaid shirt he had on when he went out to get the sugar for the peach pie. But when she started toward him and reached out her hand to touch him, he was gone.

Then, a white butterfly flew up from the headstone.

Lilah stopped, confused. *Butterflies don't fly at night,* she thought. The butterfly danced around her head, fluttered at her shoulders and circled her body. It was a sprightly and energetic one, with touches of black on its lithe but strong wings. Lilah began to laugh at the wondrous insect that had bewitched and enchanted her all in an instant. Nat was right there. Her brother was there as were all the molecules of time. The lone butterfly held in itself an infinite field of possibilities, of light, of warmth and direction, all the things Lilah needed for herself. It was a most gorgeous sight, so simple and true, this butterfly. It was beautiful.

Rose was asleep on the damp earth with Baby Girl curled by her side when a certain John and Timothy drove by in their car and slowed next to Henry's truck. These two guys—when they stood next to one another, one skinny and the other fat—formed the number 10. John was round, fortyish, and fat, and Timothy was in his twenties and stick-thin with ink black hair. John and Timothy were men beat down by the world, and every act of violence thought or done to them was what they thought about when they raged their violent wars against others.

Timothy's mom left him in a watermelon patch after she birthed him, which was the reason he was still so small and pale. He was two pounds when he came out of his mama. Never knew her, or his daddy for that matter. Grew up hand-to-mouth, eating anything he could find out of garbage cans. Fruit and vegetables usually went bad first, so his body was desperate for it and the rickets set in. Timothy's legs were bowed, and there wasn't any money when he was a boy to do anything about it, so he had no other choice but to live with it.

John slowed to a stop near Henry's truck, parked, and got out with his rifle in hand. Timothy followed at least two steps behind. It was an unspoken rule between the two men that this was the way they would present themselves to the world—John would lead and Tim would follow. John ran his hands alongside the gleaming Chevy—his stepfather use to have one just like it. He remembered the feel of the cool leather on his cheek when Josiah turned him over and took him in the back, covering his little boy mouth with his tough, calloused hands. He relived those days every moment before he got in a car, every moment after and all the little moments in between. It was the reason why John loved to drive so much—he felt a need to have power and control. He felt weak, vulnerable, and like a scared little boy when he sat in the passenger's seat, so he only sat there in case of emergency, which was pretty much never. Baby Girl perked and growled as she heard the men approach.

Timothy admired the truck. "Sure is pretty."

Baby Girl was on all fours now, growling low and strong at the men. Rose had her by the leash, but Baby kept pulling her toward Henry's truck. John opened the truck door, and Timothy rummaged around inside. John opened the glove compartment and found the wad of cash Samuel had given Lilah and stuffed it in his back pocket. Timothy found a piece of the half-eaten chicken sandwich from earlier and took a whiff. Smelled okay. But for a guy like Timothy and his history with the garbage cans, there was no discernible difference between hour-old food and three-day-old food. Even if there was mold or stuff on it, it could be scraped off and eaten. He took a bite and chewed. Not bad. A little peppery, but not bad.

Baby started barking loudly.

"Quiet, Baby," Rose grumbled back at the dog, but Baby's barking just got louder and faster, inching fast to a frenzied pitch. The sick dog was agitated now, moving to and fro. Nervous. Danger.

"Shut up, Baby! I can't sleep with you—" At this point, Rose heard the commotion from inside the truck, too. She looked up. John stood over her now, his crotch in her face. He straddled her with either leg.

"How you doing this evening?" His teeth look like parallel wooden blocks of old, dilapidated bark. He licked his lips, looking Rose's body up and down. Fearful, Rose sensed danger looming. Men like John smell fear because they know its name and live by it, and when they get a whiff of it, they strike. Rose knew this much, so she put a lid on her fear, fast and straightaway.

"Fine. Thank you. How you gentlemen?"

John smiled, sinister. "Better now." Rose looked at Timothy. Baby's bark grew louder. John bent down so his face was close to Rose's. He was still straddling her, though. "You lost? Need to find your way?"

"No. Me and a friend on our way to Newhope. Thought we'd rest a bit before we hit the road again." Rose looked at John's rifle slung over his shoulder. Baby was going crazy now, and Rose was trying to keep it cool.

"Well, we're just taking a stroll, seeing what we could see. Thought we'd take the gun, in case we saw some possum."

Rose laughed nervously. "Possum." Then Timothy joined in the tense merriment, too. Baby's barking was making her weak.

"Make that dog stop barking," John demanded.

"Ain't my dog. Dunno how." Rose searched the road for Lilah.

"Shut that dog up!" Baby started closer to John, bearing her teeth. She was ready to strike at any moment. John cocked the gun square at the dog.

"Don't shoot her!" Rose displayed a momentary bout of mercy and compassion for her new four-legged friend. Behind a tower of shrubs, Rose noticed Lilah in the distance. Lilah put a quiet finger to her lips, urging Rose to keep her cover.

"I'll give you what you want! Just promise you won't shoot her." Both John and Timothy stood over Rose.

"You'll give the pussy up? For the dog?" Rose nodded. Yes. John couldn't believe his luck—he wouldn't have to take it, she would just give it to him!

Rose and Lilah watched as John threw the gun to the ground and started for Rose.

"What's your name?"

"Does it matter?"

John's grin widened. "Guess it doesn't. Pussy is pussy, ain't it?" John started for Rose and then stopped and turned to Timothy.

"You want some?"

"Who, me?"

"Yeah, you! Who the fuck else you think I'm talking to?" Timothy looked down at Rose now, considering. Rose saw that Lilah had the gun now.

"I think I'll pass on this one, John."

"You sure? It looks good!" John smacked his lips as he saw Rose's thigh peeking from beneath her dress.

"Like you say, pussy is pussy. I'll get mine when I get home."

"Suit yourself, dumb motherfucker. I ain't never been one to turn away from some free pussy!" But just as John started for Rose, Lilah leapt out of the bushes and cocked John's gun like it wasn't the first time.

"You better get away from her before I blow your fucking brains out!"

Timothy and John shot their hands in the air. "What's wrong, lil' mama? We ain't done no harm!" John tried to soothe her.

"But I will." Lilah positioned the rifle as if to shoot, then she looked around.

"Baby! Where's my Baby?" Lilah screamed, terror in her eyes. She looked around.

"Hold on now, little mama! Ain't no need to get excited," John tried again.

"Yeah! We ain't hurt your dog!" Timothy looked over at Rose.

"Lilah—" Rose looked at her friend. Lilah was crying, shaking, as she held the rifle. Rose was afraid of what she might do or what might happen.

"Baby! Where's my Baby?" Lilah screamed out. Rose inched towards Lilah and put her hand out for the weapon.

"Give it here." Rose's voice was quiet, soothing and low, coaxing Lilah, who was shaken now, the effects of the alcohol, terror, grief and fear too powerful a combination. Rose eased the rifle from her hands. "Come on. We're all going to go look for Baby, now." Rose spat the command at John and Timothy who looked at Rose, incredulous.

"What?"

"You heard what I said! Now, get!"

The foursome arrived in a clearing. Rose had the gun cocked and ready to strike while John and Timothy searched for the dog. Lilah trailed off alone.

"Here, Baby..." Timothy's voice was high.

John tiptoed in the grass. "Come here, girl." He motioned to a thicket of shrubs, hoping to find Baby Girl. This was not the evening he'd planned for himself. Rose held the rifle inches away from them both.

"One false move and you know your ass is mine, you hear me?" Rose threatened. She shoved the barrel of the gun in Timothy's face.

"Ma'am?"

"Speak up! I know your mama taught you better than that!"

"Yes ma'am!" Timothy was obedient. Nothing like having the barrel of a gun in your face to get you to fall in line.

They looked everywhere for the sick dog. Finally, Lilah let out a wail up ahead.

Rose, John, and Timothy ran to her and found Lilah rocking a dead Baby Girl in her arms. Tears were streaming down her face.

"Baby. My Baby!" The dog was dead as can be, but still pliable and warm from its recent passing. John and Timothy looked at Rose.

"Looks like she found her dog. Can we go now?"

"Not yet. Get to digging."

"What?"

"Ma'am? We gonna need a shovel for that!" said dimwitted Tim.

"With your hands! Baby Girl needs a proper grave! Now dig!" Rose shoved the barrel in their faces, and the men fell silent as they dug the dog's grave.

Timothy, digging his fingers in the dirt, scooped out dirty handfuls and threw them to the side. *This is all John's fault,* he thought. It wasn't the first time he got himself in some nonsense 'cause John had led the way. Timothy decided that today would be the last day he would let John lead; he'd just as soon make his own way in the world, sink or swim. He thought about all the things he wanted to do with his life—that he didn't get a chance to do 'cause he was always in back of John all the time. He vowed that, from this point on, things would be different between them.

When the grave was large enough to accommodate Baby Girl, as if on cue, Lilah lifted Baby into her new home and said a prayer.

Timothy looked on, solemn. He understood Lilah's pain. Butch—his German shepherd—was his best friend. "I'm sorry about your dog, miss. Real sorry."

John gave Timothy a hard nudge for his softness. "Shut up."

Rose aimed to shoot the men.

"Turn 'em loose, Rose—"

"What you say there, Lilah?"

"I say turn 'em loose. They ain't fit to breathe the same air as Baby!"

Timothy pondered her statement. "Technically, Baby ain't breathing no more—"

Rose cut Timothy off. "Get! *Get!*" Rose cocked the gun and fired a round of bullets, grazing each of the men's asses. John and Timothy screamed in pain and scurried into the night. Rose and Lilah watched the men run out of sight. Rose turned to Lilah.

"She had a good life with you, Lilah. Wasn't no more you could do. It was Baby's time."

But Lilah was distracted. "I just seen Nat. Over there, down the way. I seen my brother, Rose. He was a beautiful..."

"Nat's dead, sugar—"

"Dead! Dead not gone. I tell you I seen my brother. Seen him in the light!"

Rose handled Lilah gingerly. "You'll meet again when it's your time. When it's your turn."

Lilah shook her head. She didn't know how she expected Rose to understand something she didn't see with her own two eyes. Lilah saw. Lilah saw Nat. She didn't say anything else on the subject, just turned around and started pouring the dirt to cover Baby Girl's grave. Rose watched a minute, then stopped her.

"Wait."

Rose took the rifle and threw it in the grave with Baby. The two exchanged a look, then, Rose got to the business of helping to fill Baby Girl's new home.

"You okay?" Rose asked Lilah. Lilah nodded and then looked at Rose's torn dress. She wondered if she came in time before those goons did any damage to Rose.

"Yeah. You?"

Lilah sighed. With Baby Girl dead, she didn't have nothing left anymore. It was gone, all of it. She didn't think she could wait her fifty-plus years to see her brother again.

The sun was very high in the sky now and late afternoon was looming on the horizon. The road was all clear and quiet—you could hear a pin drop on the earth were it not for Henry's noisy engine. A tune played, slow and lazy, on the radio. Rose drove as she took a long drag on a cigarette. Smoking was something she did rarely, but she always had a pack on her just in case the urge to do so was too strong. And it usually was before and after stressful moments.

"Those things'll kill you, you know." It was the first time Lilah had uttered a word since Baby died. Her voice was hoarse. Rose was relieved to hear her speak.

"Spoken like a true alcoholic," Rose chuckled.

"I ain't no alkie!"

"Like hell you ain't." Rose took a long drag off the cig and threw the butt out the window.

"I used to be real healthy. No dairy, no wheat, no sugar, no meat. Saw on TV what that stuff did to your insides and I just stopped. I used to carry vitamins around in little plastic bags to take during the day—wouldn't leave home without 'em."

"What happened?" Rose asked.

"Dunno. One day, I saw somebody with a catfish sandwich, and I knew I had to have one too. It was over just like that."

"A good fried catfish sandwich will do it. You miss not being real healthy all the time?"

"Nah. It got to be a pain after a while. I couldn't just pull over and get a bite somewhere. I always had to think about it, I always had to plan."

Lilah thought about the days of old when being healthy and staying here, alive, on earth, was the most important thing in the world to her. Now, she savored stolen moments where she could contemplate slipping away. She looked at the open road, nothing but open space on the horizon.

"How far are we?"

Rose pulled over and consulted a map. Only a woman who had the ways of a man would consult a map. Women generally like directions, like make a left here or a right there, Lilah thought. Landmarks are helpful too, but Rose was good with maps. At a time like this, this fact was a good thing.

"The map says eight hundred and fifty miles."

Lilah looked down and found a page of the Holy Bible peeking out from beneath the truck's floor mat. "Didn't figure Henry was the type to keep scripture in his truck. You?"

Rose smiled. "Think you know a person but you don't. You never do." She shook her head.

"You believe in God?" Lilah asked Rose.

"Don't think about it much." That was Rose. Always thinking, never feeling.

"I ain't ask you if you think about it. I asked you if you *believed*."

Rose pondered the question. She took it into her heart where she knew that she should, and it felt like nothing.

"Not particularly."

"Is that a yes or a no?"

"I used to pray a lot when I was a kid. Then I realized God wasn't coming. So I stopped."

Lilah shook her head. "You don't believe in love! You don't believe in God! Is there anything you *do* believe in, Rose Johnson?"

Rose considered the question. "I reckon there ain't."

Lilah looked at the Bible page again. "There must be something! Can't get along in this world without believing in nothing!"

"Keeps you from being disappointed, that's for sure," Rose assured her.

"Well, if you don't ever believe in something, how you ever give it a chance to see if it don't come true?" At that moment, Rose wished she had another cigarette.

"Guess you got a point." Rose watched a butterfly dart in front of the truck. It settled on the windshield a moment, then flew quickly away. Lilah didn't see it 'cause her eyes were glued to the bible page she'd found.

"I believe in something!" The exclamation was a surprise even to Rose herself.

"What's that?"

"I believe little Grace is gonna grow up to be somebody someday. I got a feeling." But the spirits always knew that Rose believed—it was just buried so deep beneath her fears she didn't know it. Her feelings of love for Grace were so strong that her fears couldn't win. The spirits were encouraged.

"Oh yeah? What's that feeling?"

"I don't know. I can't describe it. Just felt it. Right here." Rose touched her chest. She was relieved to have a feeling in her heart, after all.

"A lot of people say that's God. That's where God lives, in your heart."

"Or it could just be indigestion." Rose laughed at herself.

"I believe I seen God." Lilah looked out the window, her eyes fixed straight ahead.

"Oh yeah? What he look like?"

"Pretty brown with jet-black hair. Six feet five inches tall, with dimples..." Rose shook her head. A beautiful image indeed! "...and three feet five inches, blond hair and freckles. I know it sounds crazy, but I seen God. I seen God in them both."

"Who says God ain't a she?"

"Ain't never said he couldn't be a she." Lilah fingered the page in her hands. "Now listen to this," Lilah read:

Now a man was ill, Lazarus from Bethany, the village of Mary and her sister Martha. It was their brother, Lazarus, who was ill. So the sisters sent word to Jesus saying, *"Master, the one you love is ill." When Jesus heard this, he said, "This illness is not to end in death, but is for the Glory of God, that the son of God may be glorified through it." Now, Jesus loved Martha and her sister and Lazarus. So when he heard that he was ill, he came to the place where he was. When Jesus arrived in Bethany, he found that Lazarus had already been in the tomb for four days, and many of the Jews had come to Martha and Mary to comfort them about their brother. Jesus said, "But even now I know that whatever you ask of God, God will give you." Then, Jesus said to Mary, "Your brother will rise." Jesus told her, "I am the resurrection and the life; whoever believes in me, even if he dies, will live, and everyone who lives and believes in me will never die. Do you believe this?" She said to him, "Yes, Lord, I have come to believe." When Jesus saw Esther weeping, he became perturbed and deeply troubled and said, "Where have you laid him?" They said to him, "Sir, come and see." So Jesus came to the tomb. It was a cave, and a stone lay across it. Jesus said, "Take away the stone." Martha, the dead man's sister, said to him, "Lord, by now there will be a stench. He has been dead for four days." Jesus said to her,* **"Did I not tell you that if you believe you will see the Glory of God?"** *So they took away the stone. And Jesus raised his eyes and said, "Rise, Lazarus." He cried out in a loud voice, "Lazarus, come out!" The dead man came out, tied hand and foot with burial bands, and his face was wrapped in a cloth. So Jesus said to them, "Untie him and let him go."*

Lilah folded the page and put it back beneath the floor mat.

"You and me, Rose, we're like the sisters. Like Mary and Martha. Going to see Lazarus. Going to believe." Her voice was no more than a whisper.

"Yeah. I guess." So was Rose's.

The magnitude of the moment filled the quiet space deep and full. It was a silence that was so complete and foreign to the girls that it made them feel uncomfortable in their own skin. It wasn't a bad feeling, though, just…foreign. Rose looked down at the gas gauge. The gauge was a place of reality, a place to ground her eyes and root herself. She wasn't sure about the things she was feeling inside at the moment, so her mind quickly went to that which she could see and touch—it was a familiar place. And good or bad, familiar places are sources of extreme comfort.

"The gas gauge ain't gone down since we left."

"Ruthie said to mind the gauge. That it don't always tell the truth."

"What does that mean?" Rose asked.

"That we should probably stop and get some more gas."

The girls rode only a short while before a gas station appeared up ahead. Rose turned inside the station and cut off the ignition.

"I got money. Samuel gave me a whole bunch." Lilah opened the glove compartment and rummaged through it—nothing. "I put the money in here! Where's the money!"

"Maybe it fell out—" They scoured the floor of the truck, under the seats, everywhere.

"Men probably took it last night when Baby heard them over by the truck." Rose looked at Lilah. "They took it. They took the money." There was something about that fact that made the road before them unpredictable, dangerous in a way that it was not had the money just been there. Not that they had to spend it—it was just such a comfort that it was there.

"That's all right. We'll think of something." Lilah looked in the back of the truck and saw the bags of dog food. "Baby…" Lilah thought about her sweet old dog.

"Baby!" Rose now knew that the dog really was a gift, an ever-present friend indeed. How could it be that, in her death, a sick dog would be the girls' salvation?

The gas station attendant either came out to greet them, pump gas, or both. His name was Jeb, but it didn't seem to matter 'cause no one really cared. That's what Jeb realized. One day, he finally mustered up the courage to have a conversation with a customer, but he quickly found out that people just wanted to get their gas and leave, not talk to the attendant. That's it. That was Jeb's life. But today, good golly! Here were these women, Lilah and Rose, standing before him and talking.

"Excuse me, mister. We got these five bags of food for a dog that's gone. What can you give us for?" Rose smiled that smile and sashayed toward him. Rose near about snatched Jeb's heart out his chest! Boy, was she a charmer. In one fell swoop, Rose gave Jeb all the attention he craved working thirty-two years at the station. The way she heaved her bosom to and fro like an expert, hell, it was worth every dime of the sixty dollars he gave them for the bags of stale dog food.

Rose, victorious without effort, slid back into the driver's seat where she thought she belonged and drove. She stuffed the wad of money in her bosom.

"You got a way with the fellas, don't you?" Lilah said. Rose just shrugged.

"My mama used to say I could sell sand at the beach without ever saying a word." A good saleswoman has the world in the palm of her hands. She was good at it and she was proud about it.

"Well, she sure wasn't lying." Lilah looked at Rose admiringly. "I want to learn how to do that."

"Do what?" Rose asked.

"What you just did to that man back there."

"What you mean? Fuck him with his clothes still on?" Rose just said it like it was nothing, but to Lilah, it was everything. Lilah giggled like a schoolgirl. "You can do it. Come on!" Rose egged her on.

"No!"

"Do it to me! I'll coach ya."

"But I can't! You're a woman!"

"What difference does *that* make? Sex is sex, baby."

Lilah put her hand over her mouth. She couldn't believe the stuff that was coming out of Rose! Wow! This woman was as free as they said and as wild as she looked. Rose would not be tamed.

"Don't tell me you ain't never kissed a woman before."

Lilah shook her head. Never.

"You mean to tell me you're thirty-three years old and ain't never been with a woman before?" Rose just couldn't believe it.

"No," Lilah answered weakly. Rose made Lilah feel that she hadn't lived yet—and wouldn't—until she passed this sacred rite she didn't even knew existed.

"Best kissing you ever done in your whole entire life. Now," Rose pulled over, put the truck in park and turned to Lilah.

"What you doing?"

"You gonna kiss me."

"No, I'm not!"

"Yes you are, sugar! You're gonna kiss me and you're gonna like it!"

"Who says?"

"Come on!"

"No way!" But every inch of Lilah said "maybe." Lilah scrunched herself into an uncomfortable ball in the corner of the truck, a cover for all the weird feelings she suddenly felt inside. Was this bad? She didn't know if it was or not, but she had a feeling that there wasn't nothing gonna stop this train from pulling out of the station between she and Rose right now. Rose, slowly and skillfully, coaxed Lilah out of herself. After some effort, she took Lilah's face in her hands and looked her square in the eye. Lilah smelled Rose and thought Rose smelled good. It wasn't something Lilah was aware of, she guessed, because she had never been so close to her before. Her sweet, Rose scent intoxicated men, and now Lilah was privy to it too. She wondered what it would feel like if she tasted it, if she touched it. It was pretty and wild, a wild rose.

"Hold still." Rose cradled Lilah's soft face into her even softer hands and, easing herself toward her, she gave Lilah a long, slow, and sexy look. Lilah was almost shivering from fright. Rose kissed Lilah deep, the sexiest kiss that ever was. Rose moved away and looked at her creation.

"So? How was it?" Lilah could hardly speak. She was an odd mix of being terrified and turned on.

"It was...okay."

"Okay? Just okay?" Rose felt slighted. "Okay" was insulting. Rose felt like that was the best kiss she ever gave anybody—man or woman—in her whole entire life. She felt it tingle deep, deep down to her toes. She couldn't for the life of her figure out why Lilah didn't feel it too. Or had she?

"How about I try again? You know, just to see."

"Okay," Lilah said quickly. Rose looked at Lilah again and leaned in closer, tighter, deeper. This time around, Rose got little or no resistance from Lilah, who submitted like a willing student. Finally, it was Rose—not Lilah—who had to catch herself and pull away. She looked at Lilah, incredulous, impressed, and extremely turned on.

"That was good," Rose looked at Lilah as if for the first time. "That was real good."

Lilah smiled at the compliment and settled back in her seat. Her mind was going a million miles a minute and her heart was racing so fast she thought she would jump out of her skin. Things were going so fast—too fast. From Samuel kicking her out, to being on the road with Rose, to the goons and Baby Girl dying—now this? She didn't know what to make of it, where it all fit in, and she scrambled it in her mind to try to put sense to it.

෪

CHAPTER 17

AFTERNOON TURNED INTO NIGHT TURNED INTO MORNING again. ROSE AND Lilah were tired. Though they hadn't done much more than drive all day (they stopped by a store to snack on cookies and cakes with the spare change they had), there was something about driving that leaves one exhausted, nonetheless. Sitting, driving and watching the horizon using a crusty map and the white squiggly lines on the ground as their guide seemed like a full day's occupation. It had been a few hours since Lilah had a swig of her "water." The flask had been empty for a while now, and she didn't want to hear Rose's mouth, so she decided to hold on as long as she could without asking her to stop so she could fill it up again. But she was getting antsy, because she was starting to feel again.

"How much longer?" Lilah asked.

"We don't have far now." The moon's light reflected off a lake in the distance.

"I wanna sleep, wash myself." Lilah pointed to the lake. She assumed Rose's silence was a reaction to the previous night's encounter with John and Timothy. "Guess you don't want to risk sleeping outside in the night again." But Rose surprised her.

"Lightning don't strike twice in the same place." Lilah admired Rose in that moment, her willingness to forgive and move on without fear.

Rose turned down the steep hill to the lake's edge. She parked, then turned off the ignition. Lilah started to take the bags out of the truck.

"What you doing that for? This ain't no motel."

"Just in case we get robbed again."

"Didn't I tell you lightning don't strike in the same place?"

"Yeah, but you can't never be too sure." Lilah had Rose's bag in her hands, the one she was hiding earlier.

"Gimme that." Rose got out of the truck and went around it. She snatched her precious bag from Lilah. Lilah got out and looked toward the lake. Then she looked down at the parking brake of Henry's truck.

"You think Henry know we got his truck by now?"

"Who cares about Henry, what Henry knows and thinks! The past is the past! That's what's wrong with you, Lilah, you can't leave the past alone." It was perhaps one of the single truest things Lilah had ever heard about herself. It was the past that was keeping her in the place she was, and it would continue to keep her there if she didn't let it go.

So she released the parking brake on Henry's truck and watched as it slid toward the lake.

"What the hell are you doing?" Rose asked.

"Letting go!"

Henry's truck gathered speed as it rolled down the hill toward the lake. Rose rushed the truck and tried to pull it back up the hill, but her 120-pound frame was no match for the vehicle. The faster she ran after the truck, the quicker it seemed to careen down the hill. She got too close to the out-of-control truck, and the vehicle rolled over Rose's foot—the pain sent her reeling backwards, butt first and onto the ground. Lilah watched the truck enter the lake and sink down to the bottom and began to laugh hysterically, almost to the point of tears. Rose writhed and rocked in pain, but she never let out a sound. She held her ailing foot in her hands and rocked herself. Lilah walked toward her.

"What happened to you?"

"Doggone truck rolled over my foot!" Lilah looked at her, incredulous.

"Truck rolls over your foot and you don't scream bloody murder?" Lilah inspected Rose's foot. It was red as a beet. "What it feel like? Do it hurt?"

"What the hell you think? You crazy, you know that? They right what they say about you."

"Crazy? I ain't crazy! Letting go of that truck was the best thing I ever did. For you too! I let go. I let go!" Lilah was positively giddy. Rose rubbed her foot—the swelling had begun.

"Hold still!" Lilah got a rag from her bag and rushed toward the lake to wet it. She came back to Rose and put the rag on her foot.

"Ah! That's cold!"

"That's good." Lilah securely wrapped Rose's foot. Lilah looked at Rose a good long while.

"What?"

"I'm scared of you. You be feeling things, deep things, and don't never let on. You didn't even scream when that truck rolled over your foot! Can't trust a woman like you."

"Just can't let life stop you from living. From always pushing forward, no matter what the pain." Rose looked at her foot.

"Yeah, but what about the cost?" Lilah asked. Rose hadn't thought of it in quite that way, she just acted like she always acted, did what she always did: she bore pain and moved on. Lilah went back up the incline to gather the rest of the bags and brought them closer to the lake. When she arrived and sat back down with Rose on the earth, she noticed Rose coddling the same secret bag of earlier.

"What'cha hiding in here?" Lilah snatched the bag.

"I ain't hiding nothing. Give it here." Rose snatched it back.

"Why can't I see what's inside?" Lilah snatched the bag again, and this time she got up and moved away.

"Give it here, I say!" Rose started to get up, but the pain from her foot sat her right back down again. Taking advantage of the upper hand her two working feet gave her, Lilah opened the bag and pulled out a box of old love letters addressed "To Solomon, from Rose." Also in the bag was a copy of *Cinderella*, the popular children's fairy tale. Rose shrugged, sheepish.

"Must be Grace's. You know I sure as hell don't believe in no fairy tales."

Lilah looked at Rose, and in that instant, Lilah wasn't so sure what the real truth was. Rose wore her cynicism like a badge close to her heart and bosom, but at that moment, Lilah wasn't so sure she was seeing Rose straight. Lilah handed the bag back to Rose and sat beside her. They looked out at the gleaming lake. It was quiet all around.

Then Rose explained, "Didn't have no time when I was growing up to read them kind of books. Had to spend my time plotting and scheming on a way to survive, to raise myself up. Never read *Cinderella* until I got Grace. I like that book—I like what it say. Don't know if it's the right thing, though, for a girl to raise herself up." Rose turned to Lilah. "I had a daydream once when I was a girl. I dreamed I was in a large park, standing next to a big oak tree. I had my hand on the tree, like I was propping it up. I was scared that if I put my arm down, the tree would fall." She instinctively put her hands over her mouth because she realized all the things she said to Lilah at that moment were all the things that had been inside her for a long, long time. She wondered what had gotten into her, how and why she had revealed herself in that way.

"The tree ain't gonna fall, Rose. I can promise you that. And neither will you." Rose considered this. She was scared to at first because then she would have to admit to herself that she'd just revealed the unthinkable, that she would never be able to hold a tree up should it fall. She took her hands from over her mouth and shrugged. Ah, hell—she'd let the cat out of the bag. It was done. Just as well—it was done.

"It's important to know how to raise a girl in the world—raise a girl right, you done a good thing. A good thing, indeed." Rose looked out into the lake. She felt relieved, like a burden had been lifted. "Grace is good. She smart as a whip, but she got a lot of sass to her. Men gonna have trouble holding her down. I hope I taught her to be strong in herself, that she got choices. We ain't never without a choice."

After considering this, Lilah offered, "Sometimes it don't seem that way."

"Don't matter what it seem like or what it feels like or even what it looks like, just matter what it *is*." Rose was forceful, adamant about this. She rubbed her fat foot. "I hope Ruthie don't screw up the stuff I put in that little girl. That little Grace, she gonna be good, you hear me? She's gonna be real good." Rose couldn't stop the tears from welling up. They came out fresh, salty and strong now, rolling down her cocoa brown face in salt-filled torrents, fast and furious, one right after the other. Lilah watched her in awe—Rose was so beautiful to her then. In that moment, she was sublime. Rose didn't even take the time to swipe the tears from her face; she just left them there to do as they pleased.

Seeing Lilah staring at her wide-eyed, she asked, "What the hell you looking at?" Rose made a face that left Lilah laughing. "Hand me that 'water' of yours." Rose gestured to Lilah's flask.

"What? You want 'water'? But you don't drink!"

"My foot hurts like hell! 'Water' will take the edge off." Lilah handed Rose the flask. Rose took a sip, scrunched up her face.

"If you drink it fast enough and get your mind right, you'll have it tasting like sweet morning dew." Rose looked at Lilah, sucked her teeth, and drank it down as fast as she could. "There you go," Lilah encouraged her. Rose peeled her lips from the flask and handed it back to Lilah.

"Hopefully, that's all I'll need to get by."

"Don't worry about that none. There's a whole lot more where that came from." Lilah pointed to the suitcase that Samuel didn't pack.

"You ain't got no clothes in there?"

"You can live without clothes. You can't live without 'water.'" Lilah took a swig of the liquor. The women stared out at the lake.

"What we gonna do about that truck? It's at the bottom of the lake!" Rose asked.

"Ain't much we can do, I reckon." Lilah looked at Rose. Wasn't exactly what she wanted to hear, but it was the truth, so they let it be. "That lake sure is pretty," said Lilah.

"Yes indeed."

"How 'bout say we get baptized?"

"You know how cold that water is?"

"If you get your mind right, you can make that water feel like a hot bath." Lilah started to take off her clothes.

"Girl, you crazy!" Lilah ignored this and ran out into the lake butt-ass naked and jumped in, screaming in sheer and utter delight. "Ahhhhhh!"

Lilah dove underwater. Rose waited for her to come up. And waited. And waited. And waited.

"Lilah?"

No response. Silence. The water was still, calm. Rose couldn't take her eyes off the spot in the lake where she'd seen Lilah go down.

"Lilah! You okay down there?"

Underwater now and staring at the glint of the moon, Lilah thought of Nat. She remembered the last time she saw the Black Light that way, Nat was inside it.

"Nat!" She thought that if she stayed underwater long enough she would see Nat again, the light would turn into Nat and a butterfly like it did at the graveyard. Lilah released her breath under the water so she could stay, stay and wait for Nat again. There was something positively wonderful about the release as she started her descent down toward the bottom of the lake's floor. All of a sudden, a red-nailed hand rushed in and yanked her by the head. It was Rose, interrupting what would have been a perfect death. She was naked in the water now, too.

"Are you crazy? What the hell was you doing under that water so long for?" Confused and gasping for air, Lilah looked at her.

"I done left my child, banged up my foot chasing the truck you lost us and now you want to drown yourself? Hell no, sister! You gonna stay alive this great day, you ain't dying on me! Not now! Not today! Ahhhh!" Rose held onto her foot.

Lilah struggled to catch her breath, and after a while she said, "Do you know that you just screamed? You actually screamed!" Lilah was delirious with this observation. "She lives!"

Rose hung onto Lilah for dear life while Lilah began to laugh hysterically, pushing Rose away. The water was chest level now and Rose was trying her best to stay above it.

"Girl, get offa me! You gonna drown me again!"

"I can't swim!" Rose confessed.

"What? You can't swim?"

"That's what I said!" Rose looked at the water all around her, terrified now.

"Ooh wee! Rose, you fun! So full of surprises! Come on, I'll teach you."

"I done tried to learn how. Can't do it."

"You ain't learned from the best." Lilah took Rose's hand and she flinched. "Get your mind right." Now, Lilah was the teacher and Rose was the student—roles reversed. Rose closed her eyes and followed Lilah deeper into the water. Lilah took Rose in her arms like a newborn babe.

"What you doing?" asked Rose.

"Lean back."

"Lean back? If I got my head under the water, I ain't gonna be able to breathe!"

"I ain't putting your head under water. I'm gonna teach you how to float!"

"On my back? Can't I float on my front?"

"No! On your back! Trust me!" Rose leaned back tentatively. Lilah guided her in.

"There..." Lilah started to pull her hands away, leaving Rose all alone.

"What you doing? Where you going?" Rose lurched up, all splashing water.

"I'm right here!"

"But I need you to hold me up!"

"That's what the water is doing, honey!"

"The water's not strong enough!"

"The water's plenty strong! You just got to have faith! Floating is all about faith!" Rose took her feet off the bottom of the lake's floor. Her body slowly lifted to the surface.

"See. There you go." Lilah eased back, giving Rose some space. Rose's body was completely buoyed by the water below now, her face directly facing the sky.

"You're doing it Rose. You're floating!"

COCOON

the silky envelope spun by
the larvae of many insects, serving as covering;
any of various similar protective coverings in nature;
a hermetic wrapping or enclosure

CHAPTER 18

IT WAS MORNING. ROSE AND LILAH LAY NAKED ON A BLANKET BY the lake. Lilah had her back turned to Rose and her eyes closed, but she had never been more awake. What had she done? She had been with a woman! She wasn't sure how much she believed in that kind of stuff, but last she heard God wasn't too keen on two people of the same sex getting together. The whole concept never made much sense to her, the one about God caring about such things as that, especially if God loved everybody and we were all his children, why would he care who we love? What does it matter? She thought about the way the world was set up and felt like the truth inside her was much different than what the world said was so. She never felt those feelings for a woman before, what she felt with Rose when they went kissing in the lake. She didn't think she was gay, but she knew that the kiss she shared with Rose was one that, on any ordinary occasion, she would have shared with a man, but she didn't know what to do with it, where to put this new understanding. Lilah felt embarrassed. Knowing Rose, though, it wouldn't make no difference to her at all if she were kissing someone black or white, a man or a woman. To Rose, it made no difference at all. She even said so herself!

This wasn't the first time Rose had kissed a woman and seen her act the way Lilah acted. New feelings inside were scary to most people, but Rose was used to them—except for the soft ones. Rose opened her eyes and looked over at Lilah, who still had her back to her. She could feel Lilah was already awake. The way Lilah was breathing gave it away: short, staccato breaths, the breath of thought.

Rose lay there on the blanket looking at the wide open sky. Her foot was in so much pain, she negotiated with herself exactly how much time she would need to be able to buck up enough so that she could gather the strength to rise. She made a motion, but the pain and swelling sat her back down again. No, not quite ready, not yet. Rose closed her eyes, took a deep breath, and pushed through the pain until she found herself sitting up on her buttocks, her back resting firmly against the tree. There was a new, foreign pain now in her head, and she remembered the alcohol she drank last night. *This must be what a hangover feels like,* she thought. It was a different kind of pain, almost like her body didn't know what to do with the consumed liquid and was looking for a place to put it.

"Stop acting like you asleep. I know you up," Rose said. Lilah hated that she knew she was awake, but she still didn't move a muscle, just lay there, acting like a corpse but very much alive inside. Her eyes fluttered beneath veiled lids.

"Ain't nothing to be ashamed of." The ruse was up and the goose was cooked—there was no escaping it. Lilah finally rolled over, pulled the blanket up over herself and covered her naked body. "Don't know what you covering up for. I done seen every-thing you got. Plus, I got the same thing you do."

Lilah finally opened her eyes. "You don't even give a girl time to get her mind right, do you?" Lilah said.

"Not if there ain't nothing wrong with it in the first place. We better get going." Rose started for her clothes.

"How? Truck's at the bottom of the lake."

"We got these, don't we?" Rose pointed to her two feet.

"You can't go far with that foot of yours."

"Well, we're too close to stop now. Ain't nothing gonna keep me from getting there, not even this old foot." Rose took a deep breath and, using the tree for balance, got up and started to put on her clothes. Her foot hurt like nothing else, but still, she managed. Inspired, Lilah put her clothes on too. Still a bit self-conscious, she turned her back and guarded her naked body from Rose, who just shook her head and smiled.

The women walked and walked and walked. It was a dif-ferent sort of trip now, traveling on foot instead of driving in the truck. Lilah was the one in front carrying most of the bags, while Rose just carried one, the lightest one, and hobbled along. She wasn't doing all that bad considering a truck that weighed near a ton had rolled over one of the most vital walking parts of her body. The two walked on in silence, with Lilah checking a time or two to see if Rose was okay. But that was it. Traveling on foot made it a more solitary experience for the girls, got them to thinking more. For a spell, they stopped in the shade to get a rest. Sometimes Lilah carried the bags on top her head; there was even a time or two when Rose held onto Lilah's shoulders, using her as support while she carried most of the weight of the bags. Finally, Lilah turned around when Rose called her as she sat down on the ground to rub her foot. It was swollen now, almost twice its normal size. She was in severe pain.

"Can't walk no more. Got to stop now."

"Stop? We're in the middle of nowhere! Where are we gonna—"

"Look." Rose pointed to a sign that read, "Newhope." "We're here!" Rose saw a big, dilapidated house across the street. It was a pretty place with a rose garden, a swing and a white picket fence. Rose's eyes twinkled with delight—it looked almost exactly like the house Dorothy from *The Wizard of Oz* left and then returned to at the end of the movie.

"There's no place like home." Rose recited the famous lines from the famous movie. For a moment she was in her own personal fairy tale—she was Dorothy from *The Wizard of Oz* and she was home. Rose pointed to the house with all the glee, wonder and awe of a little girl who just received the best present she could have ever hoped and prayed for.

"What you mean?" Lilah asked, looking at the house.

"You said we needed a place to stay, right?"

"We just can't knock on the door and ask somebody to take us in!"

"We won't have to!" Rose pointed to an overflowing mailbox in front of the house. The mysterious occupants were obviously not home.

"No! Rose!"

"Why not?"

"We can't just go and squat in somebody's house! What if they get home before we get out?"

"That's just a chance we got to take!" Rose was determined and when she made up her mind to do a thing, there was just no stopping her.

"I ain't doing it. I just ain't doin it!"

"Why not? We'll be long gone before they get back. You just got to *believe!*"

Lilah pouted. She didn't like her own brand of self-help being thrown back in her face.

"Ain't that what you told me last night? To *believe?*" Rose asked.

"Yeah, but I wasn't talking about—"

"Don't matter what you was talking about. What's good for one is good for all, ain't it? Ain't that what you told me?"

This woman was really starting to irk Lilah. She needed a swig of her "water." Where was it?

"Come on now, get your mind right! You get your mind right, you can keep these people away from their house for another week or so—"

"All right. All right!" Lilah helped Rose up, gathered the bags and (one walking, one hopping) headed toward the back of the house.

"Ain't no windows open," said Lilah. "Can't get in."

"We can jimmy it—" Rose rummaged through her purse and took out a pocket knife and handed it to Lilah. Lilah tried to jimmy the window but she was all thumbs. Finally, Rose just snatched the knife from her hands and jimmied the window open like an expert. The women eased their lithe bodies through the aperture and looked around: the house was huge and filled to the brim with large pieces of dusty, antique furniture. The assorted doilies in quaint corners gave it a feminine, old-fashioned touch. There was a floral sofa smack-dab in the center of the living room. The house seemed to be part storage facility, part home and it looked like someone rushed out in a hurry and hadn't been back since.

Rose took it all in. She turned around and around like Dorothy. "This will do. This will do real nice." Rose put down the bags and hobbled over to the kitchen.

"What are you doing? You can't just be going up into folks' kitchens like that!"

Rose opened the refrigerator and looked inside. "Ooh wee! Butter beans, corn and collards! We gonna eat good tonight!" Rose started to pull the food out of the fridge, comfortable in a home that wasn't hers. It was just an immaterial matter of fact that served absolutely no importance to her. She rustled up some pots and got some seasonings together.

"You sure you want to cook?" Lilah asked sheepishly.

"I sure as hell know I want to eat! Why?"

"Well, it's just that them fried chicken sandwiches you made..." Lilah's face said it all.

"They wasn't so bad! I can cook!" Rose defended herself poorly.

"No, Rose, you can't. But you do a whole lotta other things real, real good," Lilah asserted.

"All right then. You do it." Rose handed Lilah the pot.

"Sweet Jesus!" Lilah screamed in relief.

"My cooking ain't that bad!"

"No, it's worse than bad."

Rose cut her eye at Lilah. She might be right, but no use rubbing it in! Rose was laughing inside, but she'd never let Lilah see.

Lilah set about the kitchen searching for tools, growing familiar. Rose looked around into the other rooms. She was hot, dirty and wouldn't mind a rest. She located a bathroom in a corner and announced:

"I'm gonna go and take a bath."

"All right, now. Keep that foot up!"

Once in the bathroom, Rose caught a glimpse of herself in the mirror and smoothed down her wild hair. She opened the medicine cabinet and saw the usual suspects: a razor, some toothpaste, and a few bottles of dated medicine. She found a tiny bottle of bubble bath behind the pills. She took off the top and sniffed, then poured the contents into the tub. After the tub was filled up with water, she eased her shapely body into the bathtub. The water was hot—probably too hot for most—but it was just right for Rose. She rested her foot on the knobs, out of the water, and sank down lower in the tub, closed her eyes, and smiled. It had been a while since she had the space in her mind to take a bath. There was a time in her life when she took one every day—back when she and Solomon were together about ten years ago.

She had met Solomon at the Lucasville train station—it was bustling. She was waiting for Sweet Mama and Grace—Grace was just a toddler then, and Rose was twenty-five. Solomon descended the steps from the train like a scene from a movie: he was tall, dark and chiseled, with a mass of dark, curly hair—"good hair" is what they called it—and muscles that bulged from beneath whatever he was wearing. The world stood still when he descended those steps and looked at her. She felt like she thought Cinderella did when she met her prince. They saw each other every day for three months, and for three months she took baths of rose water when they met for dinner; for a picnic at the park, or whatever. She was never a woman who believed in marriage—it never seemed to work out too well for the folks she knew who were husband and wife—but if she were ever to marry, it would only be—it could only be—to Solomon. But after three months, Solomon said he had to go, that he had found his wife and it was not Rose, and he was gone.

Rose never understood what happened. Why he came and left her life in a flash, had rocked her to her very core and made her think about the way she lived. She would have changed things—everything—for him; he didn't even have to ask. She would make herself into whatever he wanted and needed her to be. Didn't he know that? Didn't he feel that? But Rose never said a word, just let him walk out the door, taking all her hopes and dreams with him. Their relationship was like a fairy tale, only the ending was wrong. Rose wondered sometimes if it even really happened. It was all she could do to see him again, to get him back. Since the day he left, Rose thought about him just about every moment of everyday. There was nothing Rose wouldn't do to have Solomon again—nothing. She had traveled to Newhope on a bum foot with a drunk, grief-stricken girl she barely knew, squatted in a house and would wait. Wait until his arrival or her return back into his life. Her letters had come back unopened and her phone calls went unanswered for years. Now she was in Newhope, and he couldn't be far—how big could the town be? What if he would take her back and if she could have some more of the love they had once shared? Rose thought of this and more in the bath, where all her current worries and troubles soaked away and the older, more buried ones rose to the surface.

Lilah cooked in the kitchen and started singing the same tune she sang at the fish fry the day she and Rose met, only this time, the melody was more upbeat and hopeful. Rose tapped her bum foot to Lilah's beautiful singing while she was in the bathroom, which took her mind away from her lovesick heart for a moment. Behind the door, she found a woman's robe. Rose touched it; it was a blue silk, Asian-inspired bathrobe that was softer than soft and a perfect fit. Rose snuck up on Lilah in the kitchen and listened while she sang. Finally, Lilah turned to find Rose looking at her. Rose clapped her hands.

"How come you ain't done anything with your singing?" Rose asked.

The question stung Lilah, and she thought, *Where's that water when you need it?* She needed it now.

"I had my chance and it passed me by. You get one shot in life, that's it. Then it's gone." Lilah laughed nervously. She sounded like a quote from a book she read around the time she was eating real healthy. She waved the air away, as if she didn't really believe what she said was true—or at least she wasn't sure about it. She hoped. Lilah set some food on the table. "Where'd you get that robe from?"

"Found it in the bedroom. Ain't it pretty?" Rose twirled around to be admired by Lilah.

"It's nice. It ain't yours, though. Better not get too comfortable in her things, whoever she is." Lilah set the last of the food out. "Time to eat!"

Afterwards, Rose ran her hands over the bathrobe. "I used to have something this soft once."

"What happened?"

"He left me." Rose looked away. "Only man I ever loved ain't loved me back. Ain't been right since." Rose held her head up.

"What you gonna do?"

"Only one thing I can do." Rose looked at Lilah.

"He got a wife, Rose. A family."

"I know. I just got to see him. One last time." Rose's face registered real pain and was, for the first time, full of expression. Lilah reached her hand out to Rose, who flinched back. "I don't want your sympathy. I ain't nobody to feel sorry for."

"I don't feel sorry for ya. Love hurts. You ain't the first person had a broken heart, and sho' nuf won't be the last." Lilah took her hand away.

"Every woman done had her share of pain." Rose said this to herself almost as a way to justify her own and take the edge off at the same time. "At least I didn't marry a man who was almost dead. What were you thinking?"

Lilah shrugged. "Dunno. Just loved him. Didn't really matter how old his body was. I tell you, Samuel got marbles in his mouth. Didn't know what the hell he was saying half the time, just that it sounded like a song and made me feel good. Wanted to go to Memphis to sing, try for a contract. Met Samuel and... well, I don't know. Faith's gone now."

Rose looked at her. "Faith ain't gone nowhere. It's just up under the stuff where you can't see it. Don't mean it ain't there." They went on and chatted about things and non-things, but a part of Lilah had disconnected and she was a million miles away. Something was brewing inside, and this time, she wasn't going to be able to stop it.

Night fell. The women were happy to sleep in a bed. They shared it and fell fast asleep. Several hours later, the brewing inside Lilah lit a flame and a White Light shone from outside. She rose gently out of the bed—still asleep, but her eyes were wide open. The gauzy nightgown she found in a drawer and her mass of messy hair made her look otherworldly, like she was in a different space in time. A faint, drumlike beat could be heard in the distance. The house was still. In her hazy, trancelike state, Lilah floated into the living room and proceeded to knock over everything in her path—glasses, tables, chairs. Rose awoke and rushed into the room.

"Lilah!" Rose called out to her, but Lilah was too fast. She flung the front door open, and a gust of the strongest wind came rushing into the house.

"Lilah! What are you—"

The drumbeat loomed closer now and Lilah and Rose stood on the porch looking out toward the open road. He came in all white, beating a drum, with dark skin and a wide smile. It was an odd image, two women on a porch looking at a mysterious man coming their way, beating a drum and trailed by a magnificent swarm of butterflies. At this point, Lilah was accustomed to seeing the butterflies defy nature and fly around in the dead of night. All she could think was here he was, coming up the road—he was finally here. Both Lilah and Rose wondered how he knew that they needed him and that they were ready for a change in their lives, so ready that they had left everything they had known behind for a chance to be renewed. The multicolored butterflies were a most beautiful sight: wings of gold and violet, pure white and ebony black, some flecked with the richest jewel-tone yellow, greens and blues. The butterflies Lazarus was cultivating in his garden had matured under his tutelage and they seemed eager for their first and final mission.

"Lazarus. . ."

Lilah uttered his name even before she saw his face in the light walking toward them up the road. He was a vision himself, with his overalls and dreadlocks. He came because he had heard the unmistakable call from the spirits that there were two women—they were ready, it was time. Lilah thought Lazarus looked exactly the way Ruthie said he would, only the light of the moon over his head gave him a halo that made him look like an angel. As Lazarus came closer, Lilah felt the memory (almost the presence) of Nat, her beloved brother, quicken inside of her. She felt switched on—drunk with love—and the Black Light turned to White.

Be careful what you wish for. You just might get it, she heard the spirits say.

Lilah was not alone. Rose felt it too, the awesome magnitude of the power of possibilities expanding inside her. Rose opened her arms up to it to because when you had engaged it, there was really nothing else that could be done other than to take it all in or let it take you.

Their hearts burst wide open upon meeting Lazarus, like watermelons on a hot summer's day. It was a strange awakening—a metaphorical and ecstatic healing. The women moved and writhed their bodies to the call of the butterflies in the most primal and urgent way, like something resembling a dance. But when

Lazarus started to quicken the beat on his drum, the ecstatic movement of the women grew faster and more frenzied. They wept and moaned—not in angst, but in ecstasy. Lazarus walked delicately over to Lilah, careful not to disturb her altered state, and whispered something in her ear; then he placed the locket she left on the grave for Nat days before into her hands. She felt full, replete. She remembered nothing after that, just the feeling of complete satisfaction.

Lilah awoke early the next morning. Something had happened, and she didn't remember what it was. There were snatches of she and Rose on a porch with a man—and...butterflies. Was it all a dream? She smelled Nat. He had been here, traveled, and told her he was all right, that she was going to be all right, but he didn't use words to do it. Nat had come and gone and communicated with her with the voice of the dead, from the strange, miraculous place of heaven and dreams into which she had been indoctrinated. She felt lighter, different, easier. She opened her hand and in it was the locket. Wait. She started to remember. It was given back to her by...Lazarus? No, it wasn't a dream after all.

She rolled over in the bed to find Rose awake, staring straight at the ceiling. Rose's streaming tears said it wasn't a dream, that she had felt it too. Seen it. The women looked at each other a long while, unable to make heads or tails or commit breath or sound to the experience they shared in the night with Lazarus and the butterflies. It was too awesome to tell, so they never spoke about it to anyone, not even to each other. It was sufficient to know.

"I guess it's time to rise," Rose said.

And that was all that was ever said on the matter.

BUTTERFLY

any of numerous diurnal insects
of the order Lepidoptera, characterized by
dulled antennae, a slender body,
and large, broad, often conspicuously marked wings

CHAPTER 19

ROSE GOT UP AND WRAPPED HER BORROWED ROBE OVER HER shapely body. She went out into the living room. Lilah stayed back, fingering the locket. She opened it and little speckles of damp earth fell out onto the floor. She blew out what remained on the necklace and looked inside, where pictures of she and of Nat as happy kids lay side by side. They gleamed with joyful innocence. Lilah smiled, closed the locket and hung it safely around her neck.

When Rose entered the living room, she almost fell to the floor in shock. A man sat on the sofa with his hat in his hands. He wore a plaid shirt, flat-front pants, and sensible shoes. Rose was so terrified to see the man, she couldn't move.

"Sleeping so good in my bed, didn't want to wake you." Rose looked down at her bathrobe, embarrassed. "Robe looks nice on you. Belonged to my wife."

Rose was mortified. "We'll be out of your way in just a minute, mister. Lilah!" Rose started up hastily to gather their things.

"My name is Daniel. This is my house. You don't have to leave."

Rose studied his face. Was he crazy? "But your wife——"

"Louise is dead." Rose stopped in her tracks. "Been dead for a year. That's where I was. Just came from her gravesite up in Lucasville."

"Lucasville? That's where we from," Rose explained, amazed at the coincidence. At this moment, Lilah emerged sleepy-eyed from the bedroom.

"What the devil you screaming my name for in the early morning like that——" She turned and then spotted Daniel. She exclaimed, "Sweet Jesus!" and hid behind Rose. "She did it!" Lilah hooked her hand around Rose and gestured with her thumb, pointing at Rose. "She broke into your house, mister. It was all her idea! I didn't want to——"

"Hush, chile!" Rose swatted her.

Lilah began to cry. "Please don't call the cops on us. Whatever you do! I promise, we ain't take nothing! We'll replace the food we ate, and——" Lilah pleaded.

"Calm down! Ain't nobody calling the cops." Daniel looked at the empty dishes on the table. "Ya'll had enough to eat? There some butter beans in the kitchen. Tender, juicy, and sweet, just like sugar."

"Yessir. We ate 'em," Lilah confessed. Rose looked at him closely, amazed at his easy way.

"Bet you didn't make them." Daniel looked at Rose.

"What makes you say that?" Rose put her hands on her hips.

"You don't seem like the type that can cook."

At that, Rose crossed her arms defensively. "And what type is that?"

"Seem like the type of woman got her mind on other things, is all. That right?"

Rose didn't answer. How could he be so right? She was horrified.

"My name is Lilah, and this is Rose. Pleased to meet you, sir." Lilah put out her hand out for a shake. "You have a real nice house. Thank you for your kind hospitality, and being so nice about finding us here...well...I guess we should get going." Lilah started toward the door with her nightgown on.

"Where you off to?" Daniel asked a good question. Rose and Lilah thought about it a moment.

"I dunno. Back home, I guess," Lilah said, finally.

"Why not stay awhile? Wouldn't mind the company."

The girls took in this odd last bit of information. They considered it in their minds and acknowledged the aura of safety, security, and belonging cast by their interaction with Lazarus and the butterflies the previous night. Plus, Daniel felt like a man they could trust, yet they didn't know how or why. They hadn't mapped out a plan after they got to Newhope nearly as well as they did the road trip. Perhaps if they stayed a while longer they could see Lazarus again? Daniel's invitation was odd, true, but it also seemed good and right. The thought they would be found on the side of the road cut up in tiny pieces never crossed their minds. It was right that they should stay with Daniel in his house.

That evening, Daniel sent the women out for a walk; when they returned, they came back to a surprise. It was a sight for sore eyes! He set the plates down before them on the table.

"Here you go, ladies! I've got string beans, limeys, sweet potatoes, cabbage, fried chicken—the works!"

"You made all this?" Lilah asked. Rose wondered how he came to cook so well and she could barely boil water without it burning.

"Ain't nobody else in here I don't know about, is there?" Daniel bought a third plate to the table for himself. Lilah and Daniel got down to grubbing, but Rose never picked up her fork, her mind was too busy with her thoughts. Daniel looked at her.

"Ain't you hungry?" he asked.

"No."

"Give it here, then!" Lilah scooped up the contents of Rose's plate enthusiastically and piled it atop her own.

"You been eating an awful lot lately," Rose observed.

"I'm hungry!" Lilah defended herself.

"I'll say! Woman been driving for four days straight! Need to get her belly full and right!" Daniel nodded to Lilah, giving her permission to get her grub on.

"Amen. Amen to that!" Lilah shoved another forkful of the sweet food into her mouth.

Then Rose turned to Daniel and looked at him pointedly. "You know Solomon?" Lilah stopped her chewing, mid-bite.

"Solomon Jones? Sure do! He and his wife live right up the road." Daniel pointed to the window. "You know Solomon?"

"In a matter of speaking." Rose's answer was weighted and tinged with a sweet sadness.

"I'm sure he'd love to holler at some folks in town. I'll run you up there after we eat if you want."

Lilah looked at Rose with visible concern for her friend. "I don't know if that's such a good—"

"I'd like that." Rose was terse. She gave Lilah the evil eye, making her back down. "I'm going to go and get dressed." Rose excused herself from the table and went to the bedroom.

Lilah looked concerned but tried hard to mask it.

"May as well get it over with, don't you think?" Daniel replied. And that was the way of Daniel. He read, saw, felt, and heard everything going on beneath the letters and the words. He attributed his uncanny human insight to just being a simple ol' country boy. He was wise about people, places, and things that way 'cause his mama told him how to be, he thought. But he possessed more than just simple common sense. The ability to listen beneath was a skill—a muscle, a strength—developed by those who knew the importance of it.

"Yeah. I guess you're right," said Lilah, accepting his insight. She connected the thought with a picture she saw of him and his deceased wife, Louise.

"Your wife sure was pretty."

"Yes, Louise was a beauty." Daniel looked at her picture.

"How'd she go?"

"Cancer. Went to the doctor for a pain. Six months later she was gone, just like that." Lilah shook her head in sympathy. "Worse thing you could ever think of to see somebody you love get eaten away like that. We had plans, Louise and me. Start a family, get my trucking business off the ground. She stood by when times were hard, when everybody else deserted me. I wanted to give her the world. God took her before I got a chance." Daniel's voice trailed. He was positively certain he would never find a woman who was as good to him as Louise was. "It's just like they say: seems like God always takes the good ones first."

Lilah reflected on this. It was the first time since Nat died that she actually had a conversation with another living soul who had lost someone they loved recently, and it felt good. A sharing happened. Daniel understood because he knew too. "Grief can grip you good, like nothing else in this world. My brother died two years ago. I've been walking the earth feeling I'm outside, going forward by putting one foot in front of the other. But on the inside..." Lilah paused.

"Young brother dying is a crime. Crime of the heart." Daniel said these words to console, but also to help heal. *Get on with it, Lilah,* she heard him say in the space between the words. *Life is too short. You're young, beautiful and got your whole life to live.* When she looked up at him, his warm, brown eyes danced. There was no harshness to the truth, it just was. And time was running out. Daniel put his hand over Lilah's—she put hers over his, returning the favor, and smiled.

When Rose emerged from the bedroom, she looked beautiful: her hair upswept, her face made up. She wore a floral dress that hugged every curve she had, and that was curves aplenty. Both Lilah and Daniel were wide-eyed.

"Well, now!" Daniel was speechless.

"Ready?" Rose asked, determined.

Daniel drove Rose to Solomon's house in silence. Finally, Daniel glided his car to a stop. He put the car in park, but left the engine running. He wasn't quite sure why he did this, he just did. "This is it."

It had a long, winding road and it seemed to Rose like it took forever to get to the top of it where the house was. It was a green and white Craftsman with more modern touches than most other houses in the area—the paint was fresh and the flowers out front looked as if they were just bought and recently stuck into the ground. In the backyard was a swing set and toys; Rose's breath halted at the thought of Solomon being a father, but just for a moment. Her defenses were stripped as she looked at the place where Solomon lived. The ground was all but holy to her, as it housed the only man who had ever filled her dreams. She was going to see Solomon again!

"Their car is in the driveway, which means they're home. You want me to come back for you, just give me a sign."

What Rose heard over everything else Daniel said was *"they're home."* He meant Solomon, his wife, and by the looks of things, their children. She thought mostly of Solomon's wife, the woman who had the man she wanted, the man she so desperately needed.

Rose nodded at Daniel. She got out of the car, closed the door, and started up the driveway. She hesitated a moment, then resumed the walk up the path. Daniel watched as she smoothed her dress down after climbing the last step, finally arriving at the front door. She waited—and unbeknownst to her, so did Daniel, his engine still running. Rose knocked on the door; it seemed like an eternity before someone came to answer. It was Solomon. If she had taken a picture of him, it would match the same picture she saw standing before her now. Liquid chocolate beauty poured into a perfect human specimen, that was Solomon, and he was here, now. Solomon stood looking at Rose. He said nothing, then, slowly, he closed the door gently in her face. Rose stood staring at the shut door for a while. Then she walked back down the steps and down the driveway. Daniel got out, walked around the side of the car and opened the door for Rose. She sat and stared straight ahead, in a state of shock, her eyes never once leaving the open road before her or turning back to look at where she had been. During the drive back to his house, Daniel gave Rose the space, respect, and time she deserved and allowed her private thoughts and feelings. He drove in silence, mostly as a show of strength and solidarity for and to a woman he hardly knew and suspected he would love deeply.

Lilah was sitting on the living room sofa, waiting. Finally, they opened the door and Lilah perked. Daniel let Rose enter first. Avoiding Lilah's inquisitive gaze, Rose made a beeline for the bedroom, shut the door and stayed in there for two solid weeks.

In the new roommate arrangement, Daniel took the couch and the women took his bedroom: in Daniel's mind, there just wasn't another way to do it. It wasn't just out of hospitality— that's what a Southern gentleman would do—but it was good and it was right. They had no idea what a simple joy and a pleasure it was for Daniel to have company; he had been so lonely for so long. While Louise was sick, there was a steady stream of people coming in and out of the house—doctors, neighbors, family, and friends. He buried Louise in Lucasville because that's what her family wanted. They were meddlesome types, but he obliged them with a smile. He didn't need his wife to be buried in their backyard to keep her memory; Louise was all over him, all over their home. He was down, but the sight of Rose and Lilah gave him a new energy, like he was getting some of the feeling back in his soul. The women gave Daniel a peace and a hope for himself he never thought he'd feel since the day Louise died but, really, he needed them more fully and deeply than they needed him. He knew he would have to turn his attention back to work soon, so he spent most of the days fixing the house for them. There was much to be done: painting ceilings, spackling walls, fixing broken panes of glass, the plumbing problem in the upstairs bathroom, the wiring in the basement. He used some of the money he and Louise saved for the materials and the sweat of his brow to make the house comfortable while the women were there.

He didn't know how long they would stay, but he had hoped they would stay a good while. He had hoped this more for Rose than for Lilah—she was welcome too, but there was something about Rose that captured him fully and, when she left Solomon's in silence, her descent down the stairs sealed the deal for him. Daniel thought a lot about her when he was fixing the house. He surmised it had to be hard living with a woman like Rose; he could tell by her manner and the snatches of conversations they had here and there. He was a simple country man, but it appeared to him that Rose only seemed wild on the outside, but on the inside, she really wasn't. He decided he wouldn't woo her the way most men would—no, Rose didn't need a man like that. She needed a man who was so confident with himself that he could let her be all the things she was inside. He attributed his knowingness to good ol' common sense.

While Daniel fixed the house, Lilah cooked and cleaned. She and Daniel lived like brother and sister, like she and Nat. Lilah would encourage him to take breaks from working so he could rest and eat. In between, the two talked about Nat and Louise.

Rose stayed in the room. Lilah slept with her in the bed, but Rose made sure her face was hidden, buried deep in the pillow, until Lilah rose in the morning and left the room, left Rose alone with the privacy of herself. Every morning, noon and night, Lilah and Daniel would prepare breakfast, lunch and dinner for their ailing friend, only to have the plates come back scarcely touched.

One night, Lilah fell asleep in front of the television with Daniel, and when she woke, Daniel was reading the paper. He started to laugh. Lilah looked at Daniel laughing and wanted to laugh too. It had been so long since she had done it.

"What's funny?" Lilah asked.

"Police finally caught them two goons they were looking for. The ones robbed them houses?" Daniel showed Lilah a photo of the two goons—John and Timothy—who dug Baby Girl's grave in the field. "They found them fast asleep in the house of a woman they robbed. They in jail now. They locked 'em up a good long while, too."

Lilah didn't say anything about the fateful meeting she and Rose had with the men that night. She just nodded her head in agreement and said, "That's good. Real good."

For those two weeks, Rose didn't do anything in that room by herself—nothing. If she squinted her eyes but just left slits open enough so that the ball of her eye could receive the air, she could see little tiny molecules float before her, molecules that would come together, split, and combust, then float away once more. That was everything to her; it was all she could see for the darkness inside her that had inexplicably made its way outside, touched every corner of her mind and existence, colored and obscured her view. Her fairy-tale fantasy with Solomon was no more. There is something about a dream deferred, yes, but it is quite another thing to have your dreams annihilated right before your eyes, to accept that things would never be the way that you had hoped, longed for and dreamed of.

Rose tried to get out of bed several times, but could not. The weight of the wordless exchange with Solomon had pinned her to the edge of the bed and try as she might, she could not move. It held her there, weighing her down, and it was heavier than anything she could have imagined. The effort to move her body was not strong, and so she just lay there and rested. She needed to rest and be quiet, to prepare for the new life that lay ahead of her.

On the thirteenth day, Rose opened her eyes. The pain was unbearable now. She found herself on her knees with her hands clasped, calling for mercy and a place to put her pain. She looked up to the heavens.

"Hello. It's me, Rose. You there?" It was the first time she had spoken since she entered the room, and her voice sounded and felt like sandpaper snapping against her vocal chords. "I don't know if you remember me. I know it's been a long time, but… anyway, you said if we asked and believed…" Suddenly, she felt a massive weight leave her body and drop beneath her through the floorboards into the earth and she felt the earth swallow it up whole. This fall-away produced a torrent of the saddest tears imaginable. She had accepted what was true, but that didn't mean there wouldn't be a scar. This scar would become a part of her as long as she lived.

The next day, Lilah and Daniel were playing cards in the living room. While deciding what card to put down, Lilah realized she hadn't had a drink in a day. Lilah felt rested on the inside, in a way she hadn't felt in a real long time. Midway into their card game, on the fourteenth day, Rose opened the bedroom door and entered the living room.

"She lives!" Lilah called out.

"Hello, Sleeping Beauty. Get enough rest?"

Rose looked at Daniel as if taking him in for the first time. "I reckon I did." Lilah watched Daniel admire Rose and Rose receive it.

About a week later, Rose was getting dressed in the bedroom. If she took the long view out the window, she could see Daniel extracting a tree root from a rusty pipe. He was working hard, with all his concentration dedicated to the extraction. After all, the tree root was a living, breathing thing and inside it held the possibilities of many more trees. He worked so carefully and was so focused on the task that beads of sweat began to form on his brow. There was something vulnerable about the way he handled the tree root; he was thoughtful and caring and Rose thought she had rarely seen those traits in a man before. He felt her gaze. He stopped suddenly, planted the root underground and retired to the porch for a bit of shade and a cool breeze. It was hot. In a bit, Rose entered the porch from the front door carrying a tray with two glasses of lemonade. She offered the tray to him and he tentatively took the glass, looking worried—he was unsure of whether it was safe to drink it or not.

"Lilah made the lemonade," Rose said, reassuring him.

"Well, in that case…" He gulped down the whole glass without stopping. Rose watched his strong, calloused hands hold the wet glass tight and sure. She watched, too, as his Adam's apple went up and down as his body received the sweet drink. He kept his eyes on her the whole time.

"Ain't much you can do to mess up lemonade, Daniel."

"You'd be surprised at the disasters that can happen in a kitchen." He wiped his mouth and handed the glass back to her.

"Was it good?" she asked.

"That was the best darn lemonade I ever had. Honest to God."

Victorious, Rose confessed, "I made it."

"I know you did," Daniel said.

"No you didn't. If you knew I made it, you would have never drunk it down like that."

"I knew you made it. It was the only reason I could." He looked at her squarely, without a blink.

She looked at him squarely in return, then quickly looked away. "I don't like to cook," she confessed.

"Ain't nothing wrong with that. Ain't nothing wrong with that at all." Rose looked into the distance, down the road. "What you thinking about, Rose?"

"Nothing—everything. Daydreaming is all."

"Oh yeah? What about?" Rose waved him away.

"Come on! You can tell me."

Turning to Daniel, she asked: "Trees don't need holding up, do they?"

Daniel smiled. "No, I reckon they don't."

Rose smiled and they talked easy between them.

Lilah came back from the chicken farm down the road with fresh eggs for the morning. Entering through the rear of the house, she saw Rose and Daniel talking on the porch, noticing the new chemistry between them. Lilah looked down and saw Rose's toes curl. Later, as she washed the dishes, she watched as Daniel showed Rose the plans for his trucking business; he whispered something in her ear, and she laughed out loud. It was a laugh that came through full-bodied and filled with joy. Finally, she plopped herself down on the couch and waited as Rose and Daniel entered the living room. Rose felt her hot glare and turned to her.

"What's wrong with you?" Rose asked innocently.

"Nothing." She sat rigidly on the couch with her arms crossed. Rose and Daniel looked at each other; Daniel took his cue.

"I'm gonna go to the market to get some stuff," Daniel said loudly, to no one in particular and to everyone in the room. "We need anything?" His conciliatory tone was pointed at Lilah.

"Get what you want." Lilah fluffed the pillow, but she looked more like she was beating it up.

"Okay then. I'll be right back." Daniel started toward the door and closed it gently behind him.

Rose turned to Lilah.

"What's wrong with you?" Rose asked again.

"Ain't anything wrong with me. Just wondering how long we gonna sleep in this man's bed is all." Lilah moved away and started roughly for another pillow.

"Daniel says we can stay. Stay as long as we like."

"We just can't stay here forever, Rose." Lilah rubbed her stomach, then rushed into the bathroom; she lifted up the toilet bowl seat and vomited uncontrollably. Her head was deep inside the bowl as she hugged either side of it for dear life.

Rose stood back and looked at Lilah knowingly. She knew that look, had seen it a thousand times. She didn't know what it would mean for Lilah, though, so she tried to stay on the side that she wished was the truth but knew it was not.

"I told you to stop drinking that 'water,'" Rose reprimanded.

"I ain't had any water all week!" Lilah rubbed her head. Maybe "water" was what she needed?

"Maybe you ate something bad, then."

"No. Been throwing up every morning for the past week, but you been too busy to notice." Lilah hurled the last part at Rose like a missile and rolled her eyes.

"I'm going for a walk."

It had been awhile since Lilah went for a walk to be with her thoughts and without a task to be done. Not since the night at the graveyard, but that didn't really count 'cause she wasn't in a state to really know what her thoughts were—they were watery and confused, scattered like notes on a page. But somehow Lilah knew that if she connected the dots it would all make sense. Today, she just wanted to walk and talk inside her mind. It was all a jumble, but all of a sudden, something flew to her mind's surface and she remembered something, *something that Lazarus said* when he whispered in her ear that fateful night on the porch. It was something so pure that it couldn't—shouldn't—be said aloud, so she didn't. She knew it was time, time to get to getting and stepping. She set off down the road at a jog at first and then a run and finally a sprint. She ran and ran and ran.

Lilah ran for her life.

It was two o'clock in the morning when Lilah returned. She had been drenched in sweat, but now it had dried and she was just salty. Her blond hair was all about her head, so she tied it up in a bun so as not to scare Rose or Daniel if they were still awake.

Daniel was asleep on the chair and Rose dozed on the sofa in front of the television with a brown bag in her hands. Lilah tiptoed inside and Rose stirred; she got up and handed Lilah the brown paper bag. Lilah opened it and looked inside—it was a pregnancy test.

"Where'd you get this?"

"I got my ways."

The loud whispers stirred Daniel but didn't wake him. They lowered their voices.

"Besides, we got to know. The sooner the better, if you want me to fix it." Lilah looked at the test and went to the bathroom and closed the door. Rose waited outside—she was pacing nervously, fully knowing the outcome but wishing it was something else. Finally, Lilah emerged with a stick in her hands, tears streaming down her face. Rose offered her arms to Lilah and Lilah crawled into them, laying her head down on Rose's lap and crying sweet, soft tears.

"Gonna call Samuel in the morning. Let him know he gonna be a daddy. He should know."

At seven o'clock the next morning, she did just that. It was a good time—Samuel should be up and dressing for his day at work. Lilah lifted up the receiver and dialed. The phone rang and rang on the other end. Strange. She hung up, dialed again, and got the same non-response. She touched her belly and called Ruthie. Ruthie would be able to get a hold of him.

"Samuel's gone, Lilah. Died the day you left." Lilah doubled over from the news. "He came to see me just before. He knew you wouldn't be able to bear the pain of his passing, so he started you on your way. He wanted to leave earlier but couldn't 'cause he knew it would be too much for you, that you wouldn't be able to take it. He went back home and asked me to come by a few hours later to take him away. He lay down in his bed and died, so I did exactly as he asked. He didn't want me to call you, said it was important that you be on your way and he didn't want to disturb your journey, which was a sacred one as he saw it, more special that even you yourself knew. I'm sorry."

When Lilah hung up the phone, she felt the opposite of what she thought she *should* feel—it was an overwhelming feeling of love and joy, of protection and care. She knew that Samuel was inside of her, and she was happy. Lilah was quiet that day as she listened to the piece of Samuel that stirred alive inside her. She got a piece of him before he left to meet Nat. He was a good man, filled to the brim with love, and she was happy to be lucky enough to have in her a piece of him, his baby.

Rose and Lilah talked it all through, just the two of them, and then Rose left Lilah alone in the same way Lilah had left Rose alone after Solomon.

After dinner, Rose asked, "You decide what you want to do?" Lilah nodded. She had her suitcase in her hand. Rose looked at Daniel pointedly and then touched her belly. Daniel nodded in quiet understanding.

"Lilah's gonna stay with my people in Memphis for a while," Rose explained.

Lilah added, "I wanna sing. I got to sing." The declaration came out like a song, and they were glad. Glad that someone as good as Lilah had committed to her dreams.

"When you planning on leaving?" Daniel asked.

"Today. Now." They had been in Lucasville three months. That was plenty long enough.

"Today? Why not wait until after the baby is born? You know you can stay here as long as you like."

"That's seven months, Daniel. I done wasted enough time. I got to go, I got to go today."

"I can carry you to the bus station, you know. It's just a mile away."

"I want to walk. Walk and think and plan." Lilah walked toward him. "You're a good man. Best one I ever knew, except for my Samuel." Daniel kissed Lilah on the forehead and left the two women alone.

"Don't make me no difference where you go. We're one," Rose said.

"We won."

They shared a smile and a long, long look. "You gonna be a hit. You know that, right?"

Lilah just shrugged her shoulders. "I can't leave this world without trying, that's all."

"You take one step, and he'll take two." Rose looked up to the heavens.

"Who you talking about? God?"

"God, Jehovah, whatever. I'm talking about the little man up there who's pulling all the strings." Lilah looked at her, incredulous. "Had to get my mind right, I guess," Rose responded. They looked out the window toward the beckoning sun. Rose went into her pocket and took out a freshly dead, beautiful butterfly and pressed the insect into Lilah's palm and closed it tight, but not tight enough to crush it. It was a monarch with orange and brown wings.

"Thought you said butterflies needed to be free?"

"They do. They are. Just something so that you would remember."

"How could I ever forget?" Lilah picked up her bag, turned, and started up the long and dusty road.

Rose watched Lilah walk up the road a good twenty minutes until she could see her no more. Daniel came in and stood next to her looking out the window.

"You decide?" Daniel looked at her pointedly. It was clearly the last part of a question he had asked before.

"What we gonna do? Live here happily ever after?" Rose laughed sarcastically.

"It don't have to be just a fairy tale, Rose."

A fairy tale.

She closed her eyes tightly and turned her head away.

"I gotta get Grace. I'll come back and I'll stay."

Daniel picked at the lint from the sofa. "For me or for him?"

Rose considered the question. She had always been honest and wasn't going to start lying now. "I'm gonna always tell you the truth, Daniel."

"Wouldn't have it no other way." He looked at her. "I want a big family, you know."

"I can't promise you that." The way she said it left an open door.

"That's good enough. Good enough for me."

Lilah walked purposefully down the road knowing she was finally on her way—to what, she knew not, but she was heading there, wherever and whatever it was. She looked up toward the sun and smiled. All of a sudden, she heard the faint cry of a newborn pup in a nearby thicket. She stopped and bent the leaves of grass back and reached for the tiny dog, who yelped in glee on sight of her. Lilah scooped the pup in her arms without once ever looking back.

The next day, Honey Chile and Pop-Pop sat on the porch chewing tobacco and eating away at time. Honey looked up and noticed a car coming up the road. It was not a car she had ever seen before, and Honey prided herself on knowing everything there was to know in Lucasville. The car inched closer. Honey couldn't quite make out the man driving, but the woman in the passenger's seat was clearly Rose.

"Well, well, well, look at what the devil done dragged in," said Honey. She and Pop-Pop watched Rose and the man drive by. Honey Chile searched her mind for storylines she could invent about Rose—about where she had been and what she had done. Honey thought Rose looked good, but she knew there wasn't nothing good in this life that came easy.

Rose walked up the steps to Ruthie's. Daniel waited in the car, not unlike the time he took Rose to Solomon's. Ruthie answered the door: she looked good, too; her hair was down, grazing her shoulders. Her robe clung to her body from her moist skin, and her cheeks were ruddier than usual. She looked Rose over, then out behind her to the waiting car.

"That ain't Henry's truck." Rose turned and waved to Daniel, and he waved back. "I know. We had a little accident. I'm sorry." Rose's apology to Ruthie was layered and befitting the history between the two women.

"Just as well. End of a time that's gone." And with that, all was forgiven and the slate was wiped clean.

"Rose Ma!" Grace ran over. Ruthie watched Rose and Gracie reunite with kisses and hugs.

"Thank you."

Ruthie turned away from Rose to Grace. "Go to your room and pack your bags. You be a good girl now, you here? If I hear you sassing anybody, I'm liable to come correct that tail of yours." Ruthie smiled.

"Yes ma'am!" Grace saluted obediently to the familiar threat.

"Hey, Ruthie, hurry up! You don't want Big Henry to go back to sleep, do you?" Henry yelled from the bedroom. Ruthie blushed.

"Be there in a minute, baby!" she called out affectionately to her husband.

"Well then! I guess we best get going!" Rose said happily.

"Yes, I guess you best." Ruthie smiled a little, then shut the door in Rose's face.

THE RISING

advancing, ascending, or mounting;
growing or advancing; the act of a person or thing
that rises; an insurrection, rebellion, revolt

CHAPTER 20

A<small>FTER</small> R<small>OSE AND</small> L<small>ILAH SEPARATED</small>—R<small>OSE AND</small> G<small>RACIE TO</small> stay with Daniel in Newhope and Lilah to Memphis—time seemed to passed more quickly. But of course it only appeared to be that way since time never changes its pace, nor does it lag or hasten for any man—or woman. It is a plodding thing, time. There never seems to be quite enough of it, and it is the only thing one can never get back. This was the thought that Honey Chile had as she shared the porch at her country store with Pop-Pop and watched the years go by.

Try as she might, Honey Chile couldn't get no information about Rose and Lilah and where they ran off to with Henry's truck. Honey Chile didn't know why Ruthie was being so tight-lipped. But sometimes Ruthie was like that, though. Honey Chile knew that she never really went in for gossip. Sometimes, when she told Ruthie stories about the goings-on in Lucasville, she could see Ruthie drifting away in her mind, like she was bored or something. Honey Chile knew that she needed to change the subject quickly, or she would lose Ruthie's complete attention.

Honey didn't mean no harm in talking about people, though—it just gave her something to do with her time.

Since Ruthie wasn't talking about Rose and Lilah, Honey would have to paint a picture of them in her mind. Perhaps Rose went to France and lived like Josephine Baker—her hips twisting banana skirts, slinging red boas and long cigarette holders—while she entertained men who came from far, far away. In her mind, Rose would escort them to her boudoir and give herself to them—or let them give themselves to her—and she would collect their money and banish them from her bed, only to have them return again feeling duped and submissive. And Lilah? Oh, Lilah was somewhere in Africa with the Peace Corp and her old dog, feeding the folks there water and cornmeal gruel. Lilah always had a big heart and Honey couldn't see no place else in the world for a girl like her. But all these dreamings were a waste of time and Honey knew it.

Honey felt herself getting up in years now, and she wondered what else she would do with the rest of her life. The Country Store was a bore, and she'd dusted as many cans as she had in her to dust for the rest of her days. She just didn't want to dust no more, so she didn't, letting the film settle on the cans almost a quarter inch thick, so much so that people weren't coming into the store no more. There were other brighter, shinier stores sprouting up in Lucasville and Honey and Pop-Pop's place couldn't begin to keep up. Progress was moving them out. There was this new store called the Piggly Wiggly that had everything and anything you could ever imagine all under one roof, a one-stop shop deal. It saved folks time, but for Honey and Pop-Pop, it just made them obsolete. So one day at the end of the day, Honey took the

Closed sign, put it in the window and just left it there. Pop-Pop stayed current on the property taxes; that was all that was needed 'cause the store had paid for itself a long time ago.

The bus ride to Memphis was a long one. Whoever put the brown and white pup in the basket also left a wad of money inside it for its care. Lilah couldn't believe her luck! Lilah couldn't tell if the dog's quick, rapid-fire movements were due to the fact that he was sharp-smart or scared. Despite his jumpiness, the dog was small enough to ride in her carryall bag with little difficulty. Lilah sat in the back of the bus hoping she wouldn't bring attention to herself so the driver wouldn't kick her off. Whenever she felt the pup squirming or about to let out a yelp, she fed it with bits of a hamburger she purchased just before she boarded the bus. One bite every two miles or so was enough to soothe the little babe until they got to the next two miles. She looked at the pup's little ears, little mouth, little nose and little teeth and wondered what the baby inside her would look like when it came out to meet the rest of the world. Would she have a girl or a boy? She hoped for a boy, a boy like Nat. That way, she could teach him the things she never got to teach her baby brother.

She was a nice-looking, big-boned, corn-fed girl. Her polka-dot dress did little to hide the big bum she sat on 'cause it spread out on either side of her in the seat she was sitting in. She had a big, wide-set mouth with too-red lipstick, dark and matte, that she wore over the outline of her thin, pale lips in an effort to make them look bigger. Her name was Penny. "What you got there?" She pointed and looked at the moving bag on Lilah's lap.

"It's a puppy. I found him in a patch on my way to the bus station." Lilah moved the puppy away from the woman apologetically. "I'm sorry if he's bothering you. I just couldn't leave it—"

"Oh no! That pup ain't no bother to me, not at all!" Penny had a way of talking where everything she said came out like a bark. Her voice wasn't soothing, but Lilah liked it; Penny was a jubilant person, it seemed. Lilah had never met anybody that gay before in her life.

"I love dogs," Penny continued. "Grew up with 'em all my life, yes I did. Lived on a farm where we raised six of 'em. Let's see, there was Pepper and Squirt…Daisy, Chester, and Mason. And oh, can't forget about Junior!" Penny laughed that laugh. "Junior had a real thing for my fur boot. Used to bark and growl at it like it was some kind of animal. Then, he'd take it in his mouth and swing it back and forth around his head like he wanted to break its neck! Junior was the runt of the littler, but he sure had the biggest personality!" Lilah smiled at her again. Penny seemed so open and free with herself. Lilah remembered a time in her life when she was like that.

"What's your little pup's name?" Penny asked.

"Don't have one."

"Pup don't have a name! He got to have a name! Lemme look at him." Lilah took the pup out of the bag a bit, his tiny face pointed toward the sun. Penny studied him, cocking her head to the side.

"That pup looks like a 'Lucky.' Yessiree, he got the look of luck to him."

"Lucky." Lilah said the name under her breath. "Lucky it is." The dog let out a yelp.

"He likes it! He likes it!" Penny threw her hands in the air. It was such a small thing, but it seemed to give her so much joy. Her enthusiasm was contagious. Lilah liked being around her. "What's *your* name, sugah?" Penny asked of Lilah now, in that funny bark-way of hers.

"Name's Lilah. What's yours?"

"Polka-dot Penny!" Penny gestured to her dress and looked at Lilah. "What else could it be?" Penny laughed at her own funny. "What's doing in Memphis, Lilah? Folks?"

"Well, of a sort. I'm going to stay with my friend's relatives for a while. I'm on my way to Memphis—to sing." The latter sentence caught in Lilah's throat. She wasn't quite used to saying it out loud, that she was going to be a singer.

"A singer! What do you sing?"

"Anything and everything, I guess. I'm just making my way. Don't know much."

"Don't have to. If your voice is right, Penny can make a way for you." Lilah looked at her. "I manage singers, baby. All manner and types! Blues, folk, grass, straight country. You name it! If you can sing, I can get you a gig." Lilah looked down at the dog and smiled at Lucky.

"I can sing," Lilah blurted out. She didn't know if the statement was true or not—she just hoped that it was. She said it for Nat and for Samuel, but mostly for the life she held inside.

"Let's see," Penny said.

☙❧

Penny arranged for Lilah to come into the studio as soon as the bus let them off in Memphis. Lilah protested at first, said she needed time to rehearse, get herself straightened out, rest a bit, but Penny wouldn't hear of it. "You only get one shot in life, kid, and this is it. It's now or never!" As soon as they got off the bus, Penny drove them straightaway to the studio, looking at Lilah and saying all the while, "I got a feeling about you." Penny said she felt a fluttery, humming feeling inside. She said it felt like butterflies.

Penny sent her into the booth with the dirt and grime from Newhope and the memories of Lucasville all over her and her little baby growing deep inside. She was scared. *"You take one step, and he'll take two."* Rose was right about that if she wasn't right about nothing, Lilah thought. But she knew this to be true even before Rose said it. God took two steps quick, fast and in a hurry, much sooner than she was ready. But she was here now, the moment she had dreamed about but didn't tell anyone.

Lucky was safe in the studio office area, waiting, and Penny and some of her folks were outside the glass walls of her little room. It was warm inside the booth. Lilah had heard they kept it this way for the singers to make sure their vocal chords were warmed up right. The booth was small, but not too small; she figured she could lift her hands up and not touch the walls, even swing them around. It felt good to Lilah to be in a compressed space to focus and keep her mind on what was before her and nothing else. She felt like her baby must be feeling protected in her womb. Outside were all manner of knobs and wires, tubes and colored lights on giant boards, huge speakers and thick, foamy walls. It was a marvelous and good place to be, she thought. She had no idea where it was all taking her—she just knew that she was going.

They turned off the lights in the booth and it was pitch black inside and out, except for a small light in the outer room where she could see the people who were all watching her. Waiting. She felt her knees buckle and remembered Rose's confidence and thought she would have to adopt it as her own.

"Do you want anything, honey?" Penny's voice boomed from the speakers. Lilah watched Penny wave to her and wait for her response. Yes, she did want something. She would have to search her brain a bit to find out what would give her the sustenance she needed to begin to sing the song of all songs. There was only one thing that came to mind: she was parched.

"Water. I'd like some water, please." In an instant, an assistant dashed in with a glass of pitcher poured water. Lilah took it straightaway and gulped it down, fast now because she could tell they were waiting for her.

"Ready, sugar?"

"Okay." Lilah was uncertain. She looked around.

"What song you gonna sing, sugar? We got the music to everything."

Lilah thought about what she meant by this, and she was confused.

"Don't need none. I got the music in me."

"A cappella! All right then, sugar!" Penny and the others looked at her and waited. Lilah reached down into herself where all the pain and joy resided, and she pushed it out through her mouth in the form of a song. It was a series of lilting notes, and her voice soared. Penny and her cohorts listened to the rapture and were mesmerized, but Lilah was oblivious to their reaction because she was caught in her own world. She didn't know how long she sang, but apparently it was enough and so she was signed up by Polka-dot Penny and her label straightaway. Penny would manage Lilah, Lilah Belle.

Penny said she had a place for Lilah and Lucky so she wouldn't have to sleep on the sofa of Rose's folks' house. When Lilah let on that she was carrying a baby, Penny didn't flinch. Lilah was grateful. Penny made a series of rapid-fire decisions that would change everything for Lilah. Penny would pay for it all out of the money she made from her stable of singers, reliable crooners who did just enough to squeak by, but didn't have the chops of her Lilah Belle. Penny seemed confident that she could ensure Lilah's success and was willing to bet her business on it.

Lilah spent the next six months writing about the things she learned over her thirty-three years on the planet, some good, some bad, some joy and some pain. She wrote about her love for a man (Samuel); the sweet kiss of a woman (Rose); the pangs of grief (Nat); Baby Girl and butterflies and the new life inside. Lilah wrote while Penny's pals scored and composed the songs. She ate until she was good and strong and she walked—which made her stronger still—and she cut her hair and cleaned her teeth and got some clothes and—all this—while her belly swole wide and full, she wrote, she wrote it all down on the page. After six months' time, there must have been a hundred songs to sing, and Lilah didn't know which ones to start with so she gave them all to Penny to decide. When she put the crumpled-up papers into Penny's hands and told her that this was what she had written, these were her songs, Penny laughed. At first, Lilah was unsure if Penny was laughing at her or with her, so she smiled—self-consciously—and rubbed her belly while the baby kicked up a storm.

Penny held the papers in her hand like they were notes from God—she said that they were—and she regarded the things that Lilah said and wrote with great interest. Penny made Lilah feel strange sometimes, saying the things that came out of her mouth were so "profound" and that she had a "natural, God-given talent" and how honored she was to represent her. Penny worked hard for Lilah, ensuring her rent was paid every month and that there was food in the fridge so that Lilah could spend all her days and nights just singing and writing without the worries of the world. Penny said she wanted to free Lilah's mind of clutter, of the mindless but necessary things that had to get done in a lifetime. Lilah felt guilty that Penny devoted so much of her time and attention to Lilah, but Penny kept telling her it was her job. Lilah resolved to focus on the thing she did best—which was, according to Penny, singing and writing—so she could pay Penny back for all she was doing for her. She saw Penny as an angel sent by Samuel, Nat and God to see her and her baby through to the other side.

The life inside Lilah swelled with joy, and one day when she was singing a song mighty loud, she looked down to find a puddle of water beneath her feet. Lilah wondered where it came from and looked up at the ceiling and around herself; no, she hadn't seen an air conditioner nearby. Besides, it was the dead of winter, and—then she felt it. A pain so strong and sure, she thought for certain it would bring her to her knees, which is exactly what happened when the second contraction hit. They started fast and furious, quickly and without mercy, and fortunately, she was near a phone and dialed the only number she could remember in this fit of pain—Rose's.

Rose got the call in the middle of some cooking fiasco and was happy to get a reprieve. She got off the phone and told Daniel where she was going—told him to make sure Grace did her lessons—and hightailed it to Memphis, where she met Lilah. Penny was already there. Lilah was happy to have her two favorite ladies with her at such an auspicious time in her life. Lilah called Ruthie too, but Ruthie was pregnant also and the doctor wouldn't let her on her feet, said if she did she would miscarry straightaway. Neither Ruthie nor Lilah wanted to risk it, especially considering how long and hard Ruthie had prayed and worked for this miracle.

Lilah went into labor when Rose came, like some part of her body was waiting for her arrival. With Penny and Rose on either side of her, she pushed and pushed and pushed until the most beautiful baby girl came forth into the world, screaming, and with a shock of curly, red-flamed hair. Lilah was disappointed it was a girl—but just for a moment. She had hoped that she would have a boy like little Nat and wondered why her prayers weren't answered the way she thought they would be. But the momentary disappointment turned to joy when the nurse cleaned her baby girl up and put her in her arms. Lilah was sweaty and plump and Penny had to go, said she had work to do to prepare the world for Lilah Belle now that the newborn babe was outside of her. Penny left in a virtual tizzy at the arrival of the new baby she would call her niece, despite the fact there was no blood relation.

Finally, Lilah and Rose were alone. The newborn babe was fast asleep in Lilah's arms.

"Got a name for her yet?" Rose smoothed down the unruly shock of red hair atop the baby's head.

"Thought it was gonna be a boy. I don't think she looks like a 'Nathaniel,' though." Lilah smiled. She was spent from all the energy she'd used bringing a brand new life into the world, but she felt good. Powerful and strong. She couldn't remember ever having done a more noble and brave thing in her life, ever. She was proud of herself.

"No, I reckon she don't." Rose smiled. She felt the same love and tenderness for the newborn that she did for her Gracie.

Lilah looked at Rose. "Rosalee." Just like that, Lilah said it. It just rolled off her tongue.

"Who's that?"

"It's her name!" Lilah pointed to her baby. "Her name is Rosalee. Naming her after her Aunt Rose." Rose was overcome. These days it was harder and harder to mask her joy or her pain, so she just let the tears flow. She was speechless.

"Aw, buck up and stop your moaning," Lilah said.

CHAPTER 21

ROSE STAYED A FEW DAYS TO GET LILAH ACCLIMATED TO HER new life as a mother. She cleaned the house, went out for groceries and did all the things a new mother needed someone to do. They stayed in a cocoon of three until Daniel told Rose to come on home because he missed her and Grace wanted her back home, too. Ever since Rose and Lilah returned from their road trip, Grace would act out every time Rose went somewhere, fearful she would leave again and maybe not return this time. When Rose had to leave, Lilah felt a pang of pain and fear inside. Penny was nearby, sure, but other than her, she didn't have nobody else. And Penny wasn't Rose, that was for sure. Nonetheless, that was the way of it and Lilah stayed with her baby to herself, this squirmy, red-haired child named Rosalee.

Lilah didn't feel all the things she thought she should feel after Rosalee was born. She didn't feel all filled with joy and love like all the books and magazines say you're supposed to feel right after you give birth. What Lilah did feel was that the child was some strange extension of herself she didn't know how or where to place. Rosalee demanded so much attention, and Lilah was used to her time being all her own. She realized that Rosalee could not survive without her, and it made Lilah feel the burden. She felt guilty for feeling this way, so she suppressed her feelings, but then they just grew bigger.

One day, Penny asked Lilah what was wrong. Lilah had given the child to Penny to hold, and it seemed like Lilah didn't want to take her back. Penny had asked her if she had "mama's depression," and did she know anything about it. Penny assured her it was normal—her sister had it—and that it could be treated with pills, exercise and food. Lilah tried never to take pills—she stayed clear of her beloved "water" now for fear it would pull her back down into the depression from which she came—and decided to heal herself. Fruits, vegetables and fish—Lilah went back to her old ways of eating, and she took long, brisk walks with Rosalee. She decided she and Rosalee would lead a healthy life and they would stay on this path together. This new partnership with her daughter seemed to give her strength and purpose.

Rose worried about Lilah on the drive back, wondered if she was doing the right thing by leaving her in Penny's care. Sure, Penny seemed nice enough, but…well, nobody knew Lilah like Rose did. But Grace was heavy on her mind. She was having problems in school and her grades were slipping. It was a little under a year since they arrived in Newhope and she could tell Daniel was gonna be a useless disciplinarian. Rose wasn't gonna have it, and Gracie knew it, so she pulled back anytime she did anything that might warrant her Rose Ma getting in her face. Grace was getting to be a young lady now, and the two fried eggs on her chest had ballooned into tennis-like balls, perky and fresh.

Her hips were widening out like her mama's and her high, high voice was deepening to a lower octave, making her sound almost sexy, seductive. Rose knew what all this would mean, and she didn't like it. She tried to hold on to Gracie's youth as long as she could, but she could see it slipping away through her fingertips. It was like holding on to water—try as you might, it would be an impossible thing.

Rose turned the corner and unlocked the door with her key; she found Grace sitting at the kitchen table with Frank, a boy she met and became fast friends with at her new school in Newhope. Rose noticed Frank was hovering dangerously close to Grace's face in an effort to school her in math.

"Hey, baby!" Daniel came out of the back room and planted a kiss on Rose's check.

"What's this?" She gestured to Grace and Frank.

"Hello, Rose Ma!" Grace stood straight up and ran over to kiss her. Grace was almost face to face with Rose now, the girl was so tall. Rose noticed a faint look of guilt that swept quickly over Grace's face, a look Rose recalled from her own youth.

"Rose Ma, meet Frank." And with this, the boy/man rose and stood six feet two inches. He was about fifteen, two years older than Grace, and had tight clumps of blue-black curls that hugged his round, brown head. Frank was handsome, but looked too much like Solomon and Rose grew scared for Grace.

"How you, ma'am?" Frank put his hand out for a shake. Rose just looked at it, at him, then summoned Grace into the back room.

"What ya'll doing?"

"Frank was helping with my homework, Rose Ma." Grace inched back and looked at her Rose Ma, who was different now—angry and scared. In that instant, Grace knew that she couldn't tell her Rose Ma about the kiss she shared with Frank in the back of the school or the other one, under the stairs.

Frank helped Grace a lot with her homework and Rose wasn't too happy about it, but it was also clear there wasn't much she could do about it. At least that's what Daniel said. Gracie was going to be a woman soon, and Rose would have to feel confident she taught her the things a girl should know. But what Rose didn't know was that while she was dating all those many men through the years, little Gracie was observing her—observing the men she dated—and she'd decided very early on what would and would not be acceptable from the opposite sex. She had done a lot of testing with Frank even before that kiss behind the school—and certainly the one under the stairs, which was steamier and a lot more passionate. Frank had tried to put his hand up her blouse that day and she promptly stopped—mid-kiss—and just looked at him. She didn't say a word, but the look was enough for him to take his long, slender fingers from around her growing breasts and insert them back into his blue jeans pocket in hopes that she would change her mind one day.

Daniel knew why Rose was in such a huff about Gracie. Wasn't much a man could do but fall in love with Grace, and Daniel wasn't mad at Frank, no, not at all. He was a smart, respectful young man. Daniel sat and talked to Frank one night on the porch after dinner while Grace, with Rose's help, got ready for the junior prom. Frank had big dreams of changing the world as a doctor, the kind of dreams that Daniel never had the courage to dream for himself. Frank's father was jobless and uneducated, so Daniel decided he would do all he could to help Frank get into medical school. Daniel liked to meet young people with vision, goals and dreams, and he was happy to do all that he could to assist them. He wondered what he could have done with his own life if someone had taken the time to do with him what he hoped to do for Frank.

Things were going well for Daniel since Rose came into his life. She got accustomed to Newhope quickly and made artful touches around the house. With Grace at school and Daniel on the road, Rose was left with a lot of time on her hands and very little to do. One day, she was organizing Daniel's plans for the expansion of his trucking business; he'd mapped out driving routes, calculated what fuel and repairs would cost and would charge clients accordingly. Mostly, Daniel transported perishables, so it was important that he arrived at his intended destinations on time. Rose re-mapped his routes, cutting hours of driving time. This way, he also managed to cut down on fuel. Rose showed him how she'd reworked his plan, and he was grateful. Daniel's goal was to expand the business enough to hire employees to do the driving so he could lie back and spend more time with Rose. Rose liked that idea, sure, but she also liked the fact that she was good at something.

The more money and time Daniel saved from Rose's plans, the more confident she became. It felt good to her to be needed by Grace and Daniel, but she started to feel like she could really do something with her skill of figuring. For the first time in her life, she felt like she wanted to earn her own money. Now, Daniel gave her his pay every week so she could pay the bills and things, but she was starting to think she might actually be able to make money on her own with her newly discovered skill. The possibilities excited her. She was gratified that she could start a new life in Newhope with a fresh, clean slate. Wasn't nobody concerned about where she came from or her past, and if they were, it wasn't enough to go digging around like some of the folks in Lucasville. No, Newhope was a bigger town that had bigger fish to fry. She liked the space and the freedom she had to re-create herself.

So, after about a year in Newhope, Rose ventured into town with the idea of getting a job. She was all fired up about the thought. Aside from figuring, Rose's other known skill was beautifying herself. She brushed her long hair one hundred times every night and often bathed in oatmeal and milk to keep her skin soft, the way Cleopatra did. She was religious about face creams and such and no one had ever seen her without her face fully made up—including Daniel. Miss Jessie's Beauty Bazaar on the corner of Fifth and Elm seemed like the perfect fit.

"Afternoon," she said as she walked in. There were three women there getting themselves gussied up for the weekend in various stages of beautification: one was under the hair dryer (Carla); another sat waiting with her head hanging backwards in the washbowl (Jolene), and Mary sat cooling her freshly manicured hands and toes by the fan. Miss Jessie, a fifty-something woman with moles on her face, was pressing and curling the hair of a young girl while her mama waited impatiently. Miss Jessie looked at Rose.

"I'm sorry, baby. If you came in to get your hair did, you're gonna have to come back another time. I'm here all by myself, and I got more than I can handle at the moment." Miss Jessie gestured at her full shop.

"Oh, I'm not here to get my hair done. I'm here for a job," said Rose.

"A job! Is that right?" Miss Jessie chuckled as she looked Rose up and down.

"Hey, ain't you that gal shackin' up with Daniel in Louise's old house?" Carla was loud and brass. Mary swatted her with a magazine, but carefully so as not to disturb her nails.

"Name's Rose. Rose Johnson. Daniel is a good man. Just doing what I can to make him happy."

"You got any experience in the beauty business, sugar?" Miss Jessie asked.

"I ain't got no formal education, ma'am, but I'd like to think I know a thing or two about making a woman look pretty." She smiled and jutted her hip out a bit. Carla laughed out loud. "I can do what you need. Hair, nails, facials. I just want to earn an honest wage, make my own living. A woman has got to learn to stand on her own two feet."

"Amen to that!" Loud-mouthed Carla tapped her hair dryer in affirmation and wiggled her neck around animatedly. The women busted out laughing. "I swear to God, that woman come in here preaching the gospel, I tell ya! I was just telling Joseph I wanted to get a job. That man near about lost his mind, said I wanted to leave him and everything. Scared for his life!"

"Well, sugar, I appreciate that but you gonna need a license to work here. I just can't hire anybody who say they can do hair off the street like that," Miss Jessie said.

"Oh, give her a chance! She can't be no worse than lil' bit who used to work here. What's her name?" Jolene was the quiet one of the group.

"Her name is Olivia! Why can't you ever get her name right, Jolene? If I done told you once, I done told you her name a million times," Carla shouted loudly so they could all hear her over the whir of the hair dryer. "I'll never forget her name. That gal burned my scalp so bad, she made my hair fall out! I was walking around Newhope damn near bald for a year on account of her! I'm glad she's gone. Hit the road, Jack!" Carla took a cigarette out her pocketbook and started to light it.

"Carla, you know I don't like no smoking in here," Miss Jessie said sternly.

"Ya'll getting my nerves up! I need something to calm me down!"

"Your nerves been up since you left your mama's womb, Carla," Mary said. The others busted up laughing, including Rose.

Carla just rolled her eyes and lit her cigarette. She could let it dangle between her lips at the edge of her mouth and still carry on a conversation the way only an expert smoker can. She cocked her head sideways and looked up at Rose. "Come here, baby." Rose walked over to Carla. "You say you can do some hair?"

"Yes ma'am. I can press and curl your hair, pluck your brows, give you a facial, massage your feet and even take care of that mustache you got growing above your lip." The crowd roared. Carla looked at Rose and smiled slowly. "I'll have you in and out of here in sixty minutes flat looking like a million bucks. I can't promise you much, but I can promise you that."

Mary looked at Jessie, who stayed focused on the head before her. She was listening to it all.

"I like you. Yessir, I like your pluck." Carla admired Rose and took another long drag from her cigarette.

"You can do all that in sixty minutes?" asked Miss Jessie.

"Yes ma'am."

"Do it. Do it and I'll hire you. Twenty dollars a day, thirty-minute lunch and you sweeping the floor 'cause you're the last one out. Got it?"

"Ma'am!" Rose threw her bag down and put on an apron, rushing to the races. When Rose got through, Carla wasn't the same woman she was when she walked in: her hair was bouncing and behaving, her face was shiny and new, and her upper lip was as smooth as a baby's bum. More than that, Rose had seven minutes to spare from the sixty she pledged. Miss Jessie was impressed and hired her on the spot.

Rose didn't get in sometimes until eight or nine o'clock at night the four days a week she worked at Miss Jessie's. Grace took over the daily task of making dinner because, one day, Rose Ma sent her to the hospital after making some food for her and Daniel. Grace stayed home for three days after that—doctor said it was food poisoning. After that, Grace spent more time in the kitchen. She cultivated the culinary skills learned during her time with Ruthie (she was an expert at making cornbread and they had some at most every meal) and from all the books Daniel's late wife had left in the house. Rose felt awful about having almost killed Grace, so she obliged her family and stayed away from the pots and pans. It was a running joke between her, Daniel and Grace, Rose's disastrous cooking skills, but secretly

Rose felt her lack of skill in this area reflected on her ability to be a proper mother to Grace. She resigned herself to the fact that she would never be able to teach Grace how to cook, so she overcompensated for it in other areas. She felt that the most important thing a parent could give a child was the belief that anything was possible for them, and so she worked double time to instill this truth in Grace.

She also knew that children do what they have seen done and wondered what an impact shacking up with Daniel was having on Grace. By now, Rose, Daniel and Grace had been living together in the house for seven years; Daniel bought two extra trucks and hired two guys to work for him, but he still drove a truck himself. Rose more than doubled the money she earned from Miss Jessie's by simply moving it around at certain times of the week. She learned how to do this from the financial books Louise left and the daily newspapers, mesmerized by how, when the economy changed—the numbers—the rest of the city, the state, the country and even the world were affected! Numbers were important, and she wondered why they didn't teach money management at the college where she and Daniel were saving up to send Grace.

Rose rolled over and looked at Daniel sleeping next to her in their bed. It was seven years they had been living that way and it was the best seven years of her life. She was happy that he asked her to stay the day Lilah left and was even happier that she had the great good sense and presence of mind to do it.

His beard was coming in gray now. He no longer touched it up with the dye from Miss Jessie's because Rose said she liked it. Daniel did whatever he could to please Rose and she knew it and loved and appreciated him for it. After she started making her own money, Rose felt liberated that she didn't have to depend on a man for her livelihood and she allowed herself to love him even more. She looked over at the bouquet he bought her by the nightstand for her birthday the previous night. Miss Jessie made a dinner of fried catfish and lima beans, put on some music and set the two lovebirds on the porch as they talked and drank moonshine. Mostly, Rose talked about Carla, Jolene and her growing mother-daughter-like relationship with Miss Jessie. Daniel was happy that there were women who were friends with his ladylove.

Sometimes, Rose would wait for Daniel on the porch and greet him as he drove up to the house, slowing the truck to a stop as it kicked up dust. She would shower him with hugs and kisses as soon as his shoes touched the ground. She and Daniel would talk on the porch for hours. That was the thing about Daniel, too, that Rose valued and treasured the most: not only was he her friend, but he was the only man she knew who wasn't ruled by his wallet or his penis. No. Daniel had an uncommon allegiance to a force much greater than himself. Rose had entertained many men throughout the years and never found one with these traits. It made her feel safe enough to put down her armor because she was in good hands. He was wise and he was strong and she loved him more than she ever knew she could love another human being—except Grace, of course, but that was a different kind of love.

"I celebrate your birth every day." Those were the six words he chose to write on the card for her forty-second birthday flowers. When she asked him about it, he said those were the first and only words that came to his mind. It was a decisive moment. Maybe it was the birthday card or the realization of the impact her single-but-shackin'-up status might be having on Grace, but in any case, she decided to give him the thing he wanted most from her: to be his wife.

Whenever he asked, she always acted like she didn't hear him or pretended he was talking to someone else. Rose didn't need a piece of paper to tell the world she loved this man, so she had no real desire to get married. It was the same way with kids. She listened to many of the conversations the women at Miss Jessie's had about marriage and children and she didn't hear any joy in any of it. Rose wasn't sure if her lack of desire for marriage and baby-making had anything to do with being selfish, wanting to buck convention, or her prior occupation. Seemed to Rose that "the world" had designated marriage and children as prerequisites for a woman's happiness, but she just wasn't sure if that was true. She toyed with the idea of marrying Daniel and giving him a child because *he* wanted it, though she couldn't imagine loving a child more than she loved Grace.

She looked at the picture of Daniel's beloved late wife, Louise. She never felt anything but love for the woman Daniel had loved so much; in fact, it was Daniel's undying love for Louise that made Rose love him even more. To hear him tell it, Louise had been a perfect wife, cooking (ah!), cleaning, and all the rest. She was the eldest in her family of nine brothers and sisters and she was the one they all came to for laughter, help, love or solace.

Louise was a veritable wonder woman. Rose wondered if this saint of a woman was as appreciated in life as she was in death, but the more she got to know and be with Daniel—and seeing the way he quickly became a father figure to her Grace—she realized there was no way a woman could be with this man and not feel his love. No way. Rose had been "loved" by men before, sure, but there were few (if any) she ever loved back. Except for Solomon. But he never loved her, did he?

Rose rustled Daniel awake on the day after her birthday. Still groggy from the moonshine, he rolled over, eyes closed. Rose whispered in his ear that she wanted to go and get a marriage license that day, that she wanted to get married straightaway by the justice of the peace, and she wanted more than anything to be his wife forever. Daniel smiled before he opened his eyes, like he wanted to savor the moment as long as he could before putting this plan into action.

Daniel got up and got dressed—Rose ironed and starched his shirt, knotted his tie, and pulled his blazer over his broad shoulders. She reached in the back of the closet and pulled out the dress she had worn to Solomon's on that fateful day seven years ago. When she found the dress, she looked at it a long while trying to search her brain for the significance and importance of stuffing it in a ball and hiding it in the back of her shoes. She wondered if the dress still fit and didn't take long to see for herself. She washed it, dried it, pressed it, slipped it on, and zipped it up—yes, honey, it fit like a glove, just as good as the day she wore it last. She topped off her ensemble with a gay hat.

Daniel, Rose, and Grace (she was down for a visit from college) drove down to the county office to get a marriage license.

Daniel let Grace and his fiancée precede him up the stairs, counting the steps and smiling to himself that he couldn't believe his luck. He wondered what had happened in Rose to give him an answer to the question he had been asking for so long. "Will you marry me?" Underneath her silent responses, Daniel had nursed a sadness and wondered what he had to do or be or have to make this woman all his.

Grace was happy that her Rose Ma finally agreed to marry Daniel. She couldn't have wished for a better father in a man—he had taken her in like she was his own from day one. She was grateful to him for sending her to college with his very own hard-earned money, too. Grace didn't know what she had done to deserve such good fortune in her life; after her mama died, everything could have just as easily gone downhill. But here she was, maid of honor at her Rose Ma's wedding and a college sophomore. She and Frank had gone to study together (in fact, they were in the early stages of planning a wedding of their own), but Grace didn't tell Rose Ma this for fear she would be concerned about the young man distracting her from her studies. But nothing could take Grace's eyes off the prize of a political career. Grace had decided she wanted to help people the same way she had been helped in her own life and that was the best way she could see to do it. She vowed she would make her Rose Ma proud.

Rose's marriage to Daniel gave Grace a safe feeling inside. Finally, the unit they had worked on building, the three of them, was solid now. There was something about Rose's refusal to marry Daniel that had disturbed her, and she didn't realize it until she saw her Rose Ma walking down the aisle with the tulips they picked from the yard on their way to the courthouse. The worry as to whether marrying Frank was the right thing to do lifted off her shoulders and gave her confidence about her own budding commitment.

Daniel stopped because Rose did. He looked up: there was Solomon standing there, right in front of Rose. It was miraculous, but somehow Rose had managed to avoid Solomon while she lived in Newhope with Daniel. His wife, Shirleen, was a regular at Miss Jessie's. Rose did her hair often, but she never let on about her prior relationship with her husband. Shirleen would come in and talk about her great life with Solomon, but Jolene was her neighbor and didn't see anything great about a man beating on his wife. One day, Shirleen came in with an eye all black and blue and wanted to get makeup to cover it. Said she was sleepwalking and walked into a wall the night before. Miss Jessie, Carla, Jolene and Mary were all quiet while Rose succeeded in hiding the bruising, but there wasn't much she could do about the swelling. After Shirleen left, Rose went home thanking her lucky stars things ended the way they did between her and Solomon.

Rose stood on the steps and Solomon was on the clearing above, so she stood just below him; Daniel was on the steps under her, so he stood beneath them both. It was an optical illusion. Solomon stared at Rose and she looked up at him. Solomon's curly mass of hair was receding toward the back of his head and he looked gaunt.

"Rose," he said. The voice was the same, exactly the same.

Grace looked on. Rose had told Grace about Solomon, and she had seen the man around town, but this was the first time she'd ever seen him and her Rose Ma together.

"Hello, Solomon," she replied. The words came out quickly. She had always imagined what this moment would be and it was, somehow, not as monumental as she would have imagined. She marveled at what time could do and smiled. She held her hand back to Daniel, who looked at it and took it instinctively. He stepped up on par with Rose's step.

"Daniel." Solomon offered his hand for a shake. Daniel waited and watched, uncomfortable and remembering the effect this man had on the woman he loved.

"Daniel and I are getting married." Rose said this in a matter-of-fact sort of way. It wasn't pointed or intended to hurt—she was just stating a fact. Then they waved goodbye to Solomon and continued up the steps. Daniel and Grace exchanged tiny smiles as they neared the courthouse door. Rose followed with the same happy smile.

After they got the license, they went straight into the office next door and stood before the justice of the peace. Grace held the tulips.

"You ready?" Rose looked at Daniel sideways.

"Am I ready? The question is, are *you?*"

Rose smiled. The image of Lazarus flashed through her head and she realized her dream was now a reality: she had found a man to love her. She wished Lilah were there, but things happened so fast. But Lilah was living her dream too, so Rose was glad. She said yes to Daniel, and the ceremony was over just as quickly as it had begun. Grace had sent word to the salon about the marriage and, by the time they got home, Miss Jessie, Carla and Jolene were in the kitchen barbecuing spare ribs, frying corn and baking biscuits. Rose and Daniel stole away and sat together on the porch swing, Rose nestling comfortably—safely—in Daniel's arms. This was where they fell asleep on their wedding night. All was right in her world.

CHAPTER 22

LILAH WAS HAVING A HARD TIME. HER LIFE WAS SPLIT, GOOD IN some ways and bad in others. "Butterfly Kiss" (a ditty inspired by her intimate exchange with Rose) was released as a single. It topped the charts, and she became much in demand as a recording artist. Penny worked hard for Lilah. She was the jewel in Penny's crown, and she felt an enormous sense of loyalty to the woman, despite the tugs and pulls from more well-known, established labels.

On the other hand, her darling baby girl's handicap put a strain on her that made it difficult to navigate as a single woman with a burgeoning career as a singer. You see, Rosalee was blind. It had taken a long while for Lilah to realize that her little girl couldn't see. She just thought Rosalee had a lot on her mind and that's why she kept bumping into things when she first started to walk. Lilah thought it peculiar that the little girl would put her hands as far in front of her as she could in order to get from one end of the room to the next, feeling her way around. One day, Lilah was feeding her and put the spoon inches away from the little girl's mouth. Lilah noticed Rosalee using her sense of smell to get the spoonful in her mouth instead of her eyes, which stayed still and unmoving toward the other side of the room. Lilah asked Penny if she thought something was strange with the little girl and Penny said no. Lilah felt in her gut what she didn't want to say aloud. When she took the little girl to the doctor for some simple tests, they confirmed to Lilah Belle that her daughter was indeed blind. Wasn't no reason for it, just the way Rosalee came out.

It was a long road back from the doctor's office that day. Lilah stared at her child and wondered what it was she was seeing in her mind. Black? Light? She mourned for Rosalee's many losses, to see a sunset, or a rainbow, or a butterfly, since Lilah took in the world mostly through her eyes and judged things accordingly: *I see therefore I act.* How would her Rosalee be able to go through this world without her eyes?

But what Lilah didn't know was that her daughter didn't need eyes. Not to see, at least.

As it turned out, Rosalee's sightlessness didn't seem to slow her down. For her, *feeling* was really the way to go, and Rosalee used her other senses to effortlessly sense what was happening. When someone entered the room, she could immediately tell if they were young or old—younger people tended to walk quicker and more rhythmically and older sorts generally plodded along a bit, their feet shuffling low to the floor. Women had a sweeter smell than men. There were exceptions: Lilah's backup singer, Uncle Sammy (who was gay), had a penchant for wearing sweet-smelling, floral colognes that reminded him of his doting late great grandmother, the only one in the world who regarded his homosexuality as a "gift." The sixth sense is something all humans have, but in people who are deaf or blind like Rosalee, it is more developed than most. Lilah told her that her sightlessness was a gift too, but since Rosalee didn't have anything to compare it to, she just laughed and waved it away.

Lilah Belle was the opening act for the band the Hawgs and the Heifers and, by all accounts, she was slowly becoming the main attraction. Folks couldn't seem to get enough of her voice and the lilting way she sang. So full, unlike anyone they had ever heard. Rosalee was always game to go wherever her mother would take her. Instead of enrolling her in a school for the blind and leaving her at home with a caretaker, Lilah opted instead to take her daughter with her on the road—they visited places like New York, Chicago, DC, Atlanta, Detroit, Los Angeles, Houston, Cincinnati and St. Louis. Lilah surmised that life was much more than getting book smart in a school, and that Rosalee would learn her lessons, with her, on the road. The road manager had a nice place in the back of the bus just for Lilah and Rosalee, with a sink, shower, a bed and a closet. Lilah and Rosalee liked the cramped quarters of the bus; it made their growing mother-daughter bond stronger, tighter and closer than ever. Though her career was clearly on its way, Lilah seemed to treasure the moments spent with Rosalee most in the bus, after she had performed on stage. This respite from the noisy world was a sanctuary to her, and there wasn't nothing better—nope, not one thing.

It was late, and Lilah was done singing for the day. Seven-year-old Rosalee stayed in the bus and hung out with whoever was around—Lilah never babied Rosalee or treated her like she was in any way different from anyone else. And Rosalee didn't feel like she was neither, and so there was never no mention that Rosalee couldn't see. Every time the bus stopped in a different city, Lilah would leave and come back with her arms loaded down with braille books for Rosalee, and for herself, manuals and instructions on how to teach blind children to live in the world. Lilah, showered and dressed for bed, snuggled up next to her daughter.

"Hey, Mama?"

"Yes, baby."

"You ever get sad that it's me and you cuddling every night?"

"No. Why?"

"I'm just saying. Might be nice to have a daddy is all."

"You got a daddy. Samuel. I told you that."

"I know you told me—"

"Besides, I didn't have no daddy," Lilah said. It was a weak retort and she knew it, but she didn't have anything else. Lilah's daddy was a rolling stone who didn't stay with Lilah's mama long before he laid his hat in another home.

"Everybody has a daddy, Mama."

"Yours died, Rosalee. You know that." Lilah hoped that would be the end of it.

"Yeah, but does that mean I can't have another?" It was an honest and poignant question that Lilah couldn't ignore. Lilah had thought about the possibility of allowing a man to enter her life, but the truth was, after Nat's and Samuel's deaths, she just didn't think she'd be able to handle the loss of someone she loved again. Even eight years after Nat's death, it all still felt too painful, too close. She thought about Rose and how she had stayed in the room those two weeks years ago and understood why she had. Now, with Daniel, her world was right again. Lilah figured she had real, true love with Samuel, but wouldn't have it again. Still, there were times when she wanted to share herself with someone in the way only a man and a woman can be together.

Harry was the "Hawg" and his little brother, Joe, was the "Heifer." They were a country music duo who lived on the road. Joe and Rosalee spent a lot of time together, and Lilah knew it was all in an effort to get on her good side. Joe was shy and he fancied Lilah a lot. She knew it by the way she always caught him staring at her all starry-eyed whenever she was around. He handled Rosalee with such great care it just about made Lilah's heart ache. There was a time or two she felt a thump for Joe, but she let it come and go like the wind, never paying much attention to it lest it grow bigger and behave like a monster she couldn't control.

One night after the show, Rosalee and Joe were sitting side by side in the bus, just talking like they usually did. Joe had real grown-up conversations with Rosalee—he never talked down to her like she was a blind child at all. Lilah noticed that and she liked it about him. Rosalee smelled her mother nearby and her face lit up like a light. She held her little head up high in the air in the direction of her mother and waited until she sat down. Rosalee sat between Joe and Lilah.

"Evening, Lilah."

"Evening, Joe. How you?"

"Oh, I'm fine, just fine. You sounded real good out there tonight—real good."

"Well thanks, Joe. You were pretty darn good there yourself." And that was how it went. Every night for two years. Rosalee sighed and shook her head at the banal banter between the two adults and wondered why they were making things that were so simple so complicated.

Finally, at nearly ten years old, Rosalee took the initiative and felt for Lilah's hand, then for Joe's, and put them together on top of hers. "Ya'll got a lot more to talk about other than singing." Rosalee smiled and put her little head up in the air. She slipped down from between the two and felt her way to the back of the bus and into the bedroom. She brushed her teeth, closed her eyes and drifted off thinking of the man with the pretty flying butterflies who only came to her during her dreams at night.

When she first told her mama about the friend who only appeared in her dreams, Lilah almost peed her pants.

"How do you know about Lazarus?" Lilah never spoke of the encounter with anyone. Rosalee just shrugged her modest little shoulders.

"Mama, I know about a lot of things you can't see."

The evening that Rosalee left her alone with Joe, well, it made Lilah mad. What was she supposed to say? She tried to take her hand from under his, but he held on to it so tight she couldn't—or didn't—move it. He twirled her fingers in his hand and looked at them.

"You got some long fingers. You ever play the piano?"

"No, never did. My mama always said I should play, and she got me lessons with Mr. Allen down on Booze Road. But it seems he always found his fingers under my dress when I reached for the black and whites."

"Long fingers—they say it's a sign of wisdom. You consider yourself wise, Lilah?"

Lilah looked out at the stars and thought about this before she answered. "Getting there," she answered softly.

Little by little, Lilah and Joe started to spend more and more time together. There were the stolen looks across the stage when she finished her set and he started his. One night, it was late and Rosalee and all the others were sound asleep, with only the bright stars in the night sky. Lilah and Joe were the only two awake. They had just finished playing Houston, and the Texans were always up for a rousing, rowdy good time. The show was fun, fast, and frenzied, and while the adrenaline that had run through everyone else's veins had put them down, it kept Lilah and Joe up all night long. Joe sat at the front of the bus with the light on overhead, the glare of the moon and the starkness of the night giving him a sort of halo that hovered over his head. Lilah looked at it, and it seemed to beckon her. And so she did.

She took the empty seat beside Joe and sat—he nearly jumped out of his skin when he noticed her. "Sorry. Didn't mean to frighten ya."

"Oh no!" Joe laughed nervously. "Was hoping it was you. Just excited that it was is all." Joe looked at her. His eyes were a clear and crystal blue. She looked down at his lap—there was a bunch of scattered sheet music paper with its lines littered with words and notes.

"What ya writing?" she asked.

"A song."

"Yeah, I can see that. What's it about?"

"You." The statement was more a question and came out sounding like an invitation. But Lilah wasn't ready. Not yet. So she changed the subject.

"You ever been married before, Joe?" He paused, smiled a sad smile and looked out the window that held all the darkness of the night.

"Sure have."

"Where's she now?"

He turned and searched Lilah's inquisitive eyes. "Tabitha was her name, and I loved her as soon as I set eyes on her. She was what was called 'fast' in those days, far faster than me. We was thirteen when we met. Her family lived on the other side of the tracks—the good side." He laughed. "Me and Tabitha use to sneak off and kiss beneath the awning of a church. That's where we'd meet. I'd write her music—a little tune—and make up a song for her to sing. We were real young. We were happy, so I asked her to marry me and she said yes." Joe stopped the story cold.

"So?"

"So. We stayed five years like that. Tabitha paid for the house, paid for everything. I played the honky-tonks anywhere somebody would take me, gave her all the money I made. Asked her to hang in there with me, it was gonna get better. Promised her we would live in the clouds one day, but at the time all I could give her was my love. It wasn't enough." Joe shook his head.

At this point, Lilah picked up the storytelling. "I had a husband once. Samuel. He paid for everything. I gave him my love. Wasn't a time where he made me feel no other way except good about loving him." Lilah smiled at the thought.

"Man wants to do that for the woman he loves. It's enough for him just that she's there is all." Joe turned quiet inside and went out on a limb, put his hand in hers much like Rosalee had done a few days prior.

Lilah laughed nervously. "Bet Tabitha's sorry now." She moved her body, but not her hand from Joe's. "Singing sure paid off for you." Joe shrugged.

"Where is she now?"

"Dead. Got strung out on drugs. Got married to a rich man and lived on a hill in the clouds. Big house, fancy cars. I hear tell she had all the things she could stand, but ain't had no love in her life. Drugs got her so high, I guess, she was finally able to touch that sky. We always get the things we want the most, don't we?" Joe looked at Lilah.

"I hope so." He leaned in slowly and gave her a gentle kiss on the lips. The sensation was both foreign and familiar to Lilah. It occurred to her that she hadn't been kissed since Samuel—or Rose, but that was different. Rose was a woman and Joe was a man, a real man, with love in his heart. She felt his love for her, clear and strong. It was all she could do to resist leaning back and offering herself to him.

"Gotta rest up. We got two shows tomorrow." She smiled. "Night, Joe."

"Good night, Lilah." Joe watched her leave. He didn't want no more from her than the kiss itself—at least not now—and he would never want her to feel pressured. He ambled off, whistling a new tune that floated up into his mind.

CHAPTER 23

ROSE TURNED ON THE RADIO AND HEARD "BUTTERFLY KISS." The first time she heard it, she screamed in delight, but this time she just ached for her friend and decided to give her a call to come to Newhope for a visit. She was determined to cook for Lilah and Rosalee, so she coaxed Daniel into letting her into the kitchen again. After several tries, she mastered her one and only complete meal: chicken, rice, green beans and cornbread. The chicken *had* to be baked; for Rose, it was the only way for her to ensure it would be done. Four hundred degrees for an hour and a half so it would come out moist and tender. The green beans she got fresh from the market, and she made it a practice to soak them clean in a pot of fresh salt water while she clipped off the tails and tips. Maybe she'd fry up some corn too, if she felt really ambitious.

After work, she came home and cleaned the sheets, washed and ironed the curtains, clipped some magnolias from out back and placed them around the house in small, pretty vases. Lilah noticed things like that. She was so proud and happy that she was going to see her friend again after nine years (they spoke on the phone, sure, but a face-to-face visit was different), she felt like her heart was going to jump out of her chest when Lilah and Rosalee knocked on the door. Lilah was a well-known singer now, and Rose wondered if she was going to be changed by all her success; she had loved the naïve young thing who drove with her to Newhope. At seven o'clock, Lilah arrived on her porch looking exactly the same, only dressed in better made clothes. The two hugged so long and so tight that Daniel thought they just might explode on contact. He waited until they finally unclasped themselves so he could get to hug Lilah too, his old house squatter.

A few minutes later, Rosalee exited the car. Daniel and Rose stopped and stared—she was an unusual child and you could detect something different about her on sight. She walked up the steps as if she knew where and how many there were and entered the room and "scanned" it, with her tiny cherubic face held up and off to the side as if she were a computer downloading information. Then, she proceeded to walk straight over to Rose and hug her tight; she knew the height to reach, where her hair lay and the location to plant the kiss on her cheek. Rosalee took in the room, Rose and Daniel in a way that most people never do—all without her eyesight.

"Hello, Rose Ma! My mama says you my second mama. That true?"

Rose's eyes welled up. "If it's true for you, then it's true for me." They hugged.

"Okay then. That's good." Rosalee sniffed the air.

"Uncle Daniel." He looked at the nine-year-old and was impressed with the way she carried herself. He bent down and hugged her and then stepped back and spoke loudly.

"Hello, Rosalee. Welcome." He smiled, proud of himself. Daniel had never seen a real live blind person before. He had heard of their existence, but he'd never seen one with his own eyes.

"You don't have to shout, Uncle Daniel. I can hear you just fine. I'm blind, not deaf. Doesn't mean I can't see, though." Rosalee laughed devilishly. Lilah looked at her child for a moment like it was the first time. She remembered she had heard that before: *Just because you can't see it, doesn't mean it isn't there.* She had heard it from the spirits long ago, the voices she heard but couldn't see, the ones that told her about reality and who she was, only they didn't have a face, a body or a name. Lilah looked at her daughter who talked like the spirits she hadn't heard from in a long time and wondered if Rosalee came from the same place they did. Or was it Rosalee's voice she was hearing even before she was born? Rose and Daniel moved out of the way while Rosalee took in her new surroundings in the way that only Rosalee could.

"You don't have to move," said Lilah. "In fact, best that you don't. The world won't move for Rosalee because she's blind. I taught her that. She knows how to get around on her own." Rose and Daniel watched the little girl make her way around chairs, pick up the vase on the table, and smell the flowers; she even smoothed out the corners of the pillow on the couch before she plopped down to rest herself.

"You got some water, Rose? Rosalee needs lots of it." Rose thought the statement odd. She wanted to inquire, but she didn't ask Lilah anything more.

"Of course." Lilah followed Rose into the kitchen, where she remained quiet, in the way most people did when they encountered

Rosalee for the first time. Rose poured a glass of water from the pitcher in the fridge and handed it to Lilah.

"Why don't you give it to her? It'll mean a lot more coming from you." Rose didn't know what that meant either, but she did as she was told. She walked back into the living room with the glass of water in her hand. Should she offer Rosalee the water? Put it in her hand or put it on the table?

"Put it on the table. Rosalee will know where it is and drink it when she's ready." Rose didn't know how Lilah could hear her thoughts, but again, she did exactly as she was told. She walked a few steps toward Rosalee and set the glass of water on the table.

"Thank you." Rosalee pointed her little head heavenward and put her ear toward the water; then, she turned straight toward it, placed her tiny fingers firmly around the glass, picked it up and drank it. Rosalee drank it down like she was in the Sahara. Daniel and Rose looked at her, mesmerized.

"Why don't you and me go into the kitchen Rose, talk women stuff. We got a lot of catching up to do, huh?" Rose finally took her eyes off Rosalee and looked at Lilah, whose hand was offered out to Rose. They walked into the kitchen, hands clasped.

Daniel hung back, studying Rosalee from afar. My God, she was odd, he thought. He was downright spooked by her; she looked fragile with her pale skin and red hair, but the truth was, Rosalee was as sturdy as they come. She raised her little head again in the air, turned it toward Daniel, and smiled. Daniel was visibly shaken as Rosalee appeared to be looking straight into him with her sightless eyes, but he knew this couldn't be possible—could it? She tapped the seat next to her on the couch. Daniel followed like a calling.

"Anything you want to ask me, Uncle Daniel?"

"No. Why do you ask me that?" Daniel questioned her defensively. "Do you want some more water?"

"That's two questions!" Rosalee smiled. "No, I've had all I can drink for now. Maybe later." There was a pause. In it, Daniel mustered up the courage to ask the girl what was really on his mind.

"Can't you see nothing?" It was a hard thing to grasp, that her eyes were open and she still couldn't see. Daniel waved his hand across her face.

"Nope. But I can feel the wind from your hand and the smell of you." Rosalee then waved her hands in front of him in exactly the way that Daniel had.

"Don't you know any colors?" he asked.

"Colors?"

"Yeah! Like blue, and orange, and red." Daniel asked the girl this, but the question was tinged with sadness. He felt sorry for her, that she would never get to see colors.

"I dunno if I need to see colors, Uncle Daniel."

"Sure you do! Girl, you need to try and fix your eyes to see the sunset or a sunrise! The rainbow in the sky after a rainfall! You got to—you just got to—or you ain't really living!" The statement came out passionate and frenzied, more than Daniel even expected it to come out of himself. He didn't know why he was so adamant about Rosalee seeing, he just knew that he instantly felt protective of her and wanted so much for her to experience these important things. She could get around the table and pick up a glass of water, sure, but how would she maneuver in this life without eyes to see the pits and snares the world held in wait for her? It was just too much for his heart and mind to bear, and he felt he had to shake some sense into this little girl who didn't know what she had signed up for. "People can steal from you, Rosalee, and you'd never even know it."

"The things you can see have as much value as you decide to give them, Uncle Daniel." She said it as if she were a teacher and he was a student. "Just because you can't see something with your eyes or touch it with your hands doesn't mean it ain't real. In fact, it's realer than real. It's the only thing that can't change—it's the only truth you can rely on above all else. Most things that count—really count—are the ones you *don't* see. Your eyes can betray you, but your heart never will."

"That's what they say, but how can you prove it? Where are the facts?" Daniel persisted.

"There are none that you can see."

"So then, it doesn't exist!"

"So then the feeling Aunt Rose gives you when you wake up in the morning and see her face, doesn't that exist?"

"A feeling is a feeling! They come and they go!"

"Because you let them in and out; you feel it, and your eyes and mind rush off to something else. Doesn't mean that the love is gone, does it?" Daniel knitted his brow. He didn't know what the hell Rosalee was talking about, but he knew there was some part of him that did understand. He tried to make sense of the things she said, but couldn't.

"Some things you can't put in words." Rosalee tilted her head toward him.

"Let me go see what they're doing in the kitchen," was all he could say. He walked off, leaving Rosalee to sit in the living room by herself.

Rose and Lilah were startled when Daniel burst into the kitchen. He had a strange look on his face as they waited for him to deliver whatever message that had motivated the excited entrance.

"Baby, what is it?" Rose waited.

"Rosalee," Daniel said almost to himself. They could tell he was searching his mind for the answers—or the questions.

"What about her, baby? She okay?"

"She's—" Lilah looked at him. Men often had this reaction after an encounter with Rosalee. They were given to facts, figures, quantifications—things that were tangible, things they could touch. Rosalee had this effect on virtually every man she met—every man except Joe. That was one of the ways she knew he was destined to fit in with her life.

"She saying deep things that stir you up?" Lilah knew her child well. She almost felt that Rosalee took pleasure in spooking people with the things she knew; Lilah could tell that it made Rosalee feel confident, almost triumphant. She would have to teach Rosalee to be more responsible with her gift and judicious about the show-and-tell aspect of it. Not everybody could handle it—nor should they.

"She's an—interesting young person," was all Daniel would say. He was working something around in his mind, and after a while he left the two old friends and retreated to the back bedroom to be alone with his thoughts.

"Is it hard? Her being blind and all?" Rose finally asked.

"Hardly ever think about it." And that was all Lilah said on the matter. It gave Rose permission to change the subject to one she felt more comfortable with.

"So tell me what it's like to be a star!"

"Please! I ain't hardly no *star.*"

"Sure you are! I saw on the TV that 'Butterfly Kiss' sold thirty thousand copies in one hour. Thirty thousand copies!" Rose swelled with pride for her friend. Lilah saw that Rose had that look about herself that people developed when they realized that Lilah was the same woman who sang the hit song everybody loved. This distinction always made Lilah feel like they were talking about another woman, not her. She didn't want this fact to come between them, so she did what she had learned to do: she took the power out of the "fame" concept and let people feel at ease that it was still just her, just plain ol' Lilah.

"It's a song I wrote that caught on somehow—it could happen to anybody. Wasn't nothing special." This was the truth—yes, it was a song Lilah created, but it was not true that it could have happened to anyone. It could have only happened to her, with that song at that time—a fact that Lilah was reluctant to accept. It made her so uncomfortable that she slowly developed a dismissive attitude toward her fame and popularity. Lilah was dog tired after eleven years on the road. She had written and sung many songs on the road many times, but "Butterfly Kiss," her first, was the one she was most identified with. She wanted to step back from touring. This wasn't something she told a lot of people because, when she did, she got so many protests. "How could a famous singer suddenly no longer want to be famous? Isn't that the thing most people live for all their lives? To be rich and famous?" Lilah didn't know what other people lived for, but singing songs had little or nothing to do with her reason to live anymore. That initial drive was an internal need that was quenched and filled long ago. Singing was less about the approval of others and more about her own of herself. It was hard to make people understand this, so she rarely discussed it. What was the point? She started a new subject.

"How's Daniel's trucking business going?"

"Great! Was taking these classes for business until the teacher started making eyes at me." Rose rolled her eyes.

"Ain't surprised. Ain't surprised one bit…"

"Yeah, well, I'm a married woman now. Don't do them kinds of things." Rose smiled. "Anyhoo, I taught myself how to double our money by investing. Now, me and the women in the shop have an investment club where we pick companies to invest in."

"Do tell!"

"I don't do hair and nails no more. Miss Jessie is getting on in years, so I take care of her books—we even opening up another store in the next town! Sometimes I go with Daniel on the road to make deliveries or pickups. It always reminds me of the time we took our trip here to Newhope."

"That seems like a lifetime ago."

The women fell silent, remembering.

Rose was especially proud that she had taught Shirleen to double her money. See, Shirleen was planning to leave Solomon and Rose was teaching her how to make money so she'd have it to take care of herself and her two kids. Rose considered her skill. Figuring wasn't thought of as a real feminine thing. She heard her mother's voice in her head, saying, *There she goes again, acting like a man,* and the clucking of the mouth and the shaking of the head that came shortly after. It was hard at first, but Rose learned to ignore these thoughts as they came; she never could stop them, just didn't pay them as much time, energy, and attention as she used to. Eventually, they went away on their own.

"Looks like you and Daniel doing real good together."

Rose grinned. "I love him, Lilah. Never thought I would love somebody again, but I do. I just do! It's a different, better, sweeter kind of love."

"That's good, Rose."

"Yes, it is. He's good to me and good for me."

"Can't find a better combination that that." There was a quiet spell between them for a bit, and Lilah began to fidget with her eyes.

"You give Joe any yet?"

"I can't believe you said that! You still nasty—nasty as ever!"

"Dunno why you torturing that man. You need to live, Lilah."

"I *am* living!"

"If what you say is true, that man loves you. Loves you *and* Rosalee. Just wants to get a little loving back is all."

"Oh, who's talking now! Sounds like something I told you about Daniel years ago."

"It's bad when you get your own words thrown back at you, ain't it?" Rose laughed.

"You know I ain't the type to go around sleeping with everybody."

"Everybody? How 'bout nobody! You better use that coochie—make sure it's still there." Lilah had a stern look on her face, but when Rose said this she couldn't stifle her own laugh.

"He ain't gonna die, Lilah," Rose said gently.

Lilah took this in. "We all die, Rose."

"Well, he ain't gonna die because you gave him some! If what you say is true, best to give him a taste before he finds himself in the ground. Least you can do—that man been loving you all these years."

Lilah turned away, humphing to herself. As crass as Rose was talking about sex, she knew she was really talking about love. Lilah *had* been thinking more about love. What she felt sure of was the love she shared with Rosalee and her dog Lucky.

But what about Joe?

She never felt much love from her parents. Her daddy was busy rolling his stones and her mama never seemed to put herself out over her children. That's how she and Nat had become so close, because they had no one else to love on. Nat and then Samuel were the two men who loved her, and she felt loved by them still, though the power of the connection grew more distant with time. Lilah felt a kind of love when she was on stage singing. There was the love of joining up with the music, the song. And the audience's response, their appreciation for her, also felt something like a form of love. Lilah felt the bulk of her love from the place where Nat and Samuel were, the place where Rosalee went frequently and communed with daily. It was a love that held her tightly even when she felt weak—especially when she felt weak. She couldn't see it, feel it, taste it, or touch it, but it was just enough. It was the love of God.

But what about Joe?

"Daniel's been pestering me about having babies," Rose blurted out.

"Babies!"

"Can you believe it? I'm forty-four years old. What the hell am I gonna do with a baby at this age?"

"You gonna love it! It's gonna love you!" Lilah proclaimed. Rose rolled her eyes.

"I missed my period."

"You missed your period—you missed it! Hot diggity dawg, Rose, you gonna have a baby! We gonna have a baby! Ha!" Lilah was ecstatic.

Rose shushed her. "Dunno for sure. Wanted to wait until you got here. Take the test and see."

"Pee on the stick?"

"Yeah. See if it turns blue or not."

"Just like old times." The women smiled at each other. "Daniel's gonna be so happy," Lilah said.

"Yeah. Yeah, he will be." Rose smiled at the thought of telling her husband he was finally going to be a daddy. It was the thing about all this that she looked forward to the most. Daniel had loved her so good, so long and so strong, she felt it was the least she could do for him, and she was happy that she could.

"You got your fairy tale—your Cinderella ending—happily ever after. You know that?"

"Yes, I do. I know it."

"Good. Good, I'm glad you do."

CHAPTER 24

ROSALEE SAT ON THE COUCH ALONE. SHE COCKED HER HEAD slightly to the sky and listened as Rose and Lilah entered the room. Her face was contorted tightly in sorrow. She looked down, opened her hand and held out her palm, holding a dead butterfly. She fingered the torn, delicate wings and began to cry. She quickly grew into a state of complete and utter despair.

"Rosalee! What is it, baby? What did you—see?"

"Mama!" The child shook her head as if she were trying to shake an image out her mind. Rosalee "looked" at Rose and hugged her tight. "I'm sorry, Rose Ma. So sorry."

The next morning, there were clouds in the sky. Lilah stayed up most of the night with Rosalee because she was spooked by the little girl's statement to Rose. She tried not to think about it, tried not to let it bother her, but she had to admit that it had. What had Rosalee seen that was bad? Maybe it was nothing, nothing at all, a false alarm or a warning Rosalee got that was really for someone else, not her. Lilah knew that things like that happened sometimes with people like Rosalee, like wires getting crossed. Lilah slept most of the night with the knowledge that whatever was going to happen was going to keep her in Newhope longer than she had planned. Whatever Rosalee had seen, Lilah was going to help Rose through it.

Daniel made them all a breakfast of home fries, eggs, biscuits and gravy, and then he went on his way to work. Afterward, Rose and Lilah headed over to the market and bought a pregnancy test. They crowded into the tiny bathroom while Lilah held the stick underneath Rose so that she could pee squarely on it. The bar turned blue almost immediately. Rose was gonna be a mama! The women hugged each other real tight, separated only by the new, young life growing inside between them.

Rose received a phone call that Daniel had been in an accident shortly after Rose found out she was pregnant. He had entered the freeway, merging lanes, when a bigger truck collided with his, knocking his two-ton truck over—twice—on its head. Daniel's truck burst into flames when it hit the bottom of a wooded, dry embankment. It took ten men to put out the blaze and then cut poor Daniel out of the truck, his searing flesh stuck to the bottom of his seat. His seatbelt was still on when they found him. The doctors said it was one of the rare instances when not wearing the belt might have saved him. Without the belt, he might have been thrown safely free from the vehicle.

Rose fell to her knees and dropped the phone when they told her he was in the emergency room. She rushed outside to the car while Lilah got directions and drove them to the hospital where Daniel lay. He was a remnant of his former self: the joyful, strong man was reduced to a shell of a being, with the smell of still-seared flesh an overpowering reminder of the vulnerability of the human body. Lilah canceled her tour dates and stayed with Rose. Rosalee went eerily silent, as if she felt responsible somehow for what had happened to Daniel. She didn't understand why these powerful forebodings, almost like prophecies, would come to her before they actually happened in real life. She knew Lilah referred to this knowing as a "gift," but lately, Rosalee had been thinking it was more of a curse.

Rose and Lilah stayed in the hospital room with Daniel for three straight months; three months, days and nights into days again, standing vigil by a man who was in so many ways no longer there. Rose grew content to have any piece of him that God let her have and she rocked herself beside his bed day and night. Grace came down and joined them for a spell. She was running for a district leader position in DC (which was where she and Frank had settled after college and got married), but she left the campaign straightaway to be with her Rose Ma. After Rose and Daniel sent her off to American University, she began calling Daniel "Daddy." Her biological dad had left the scene long ago and she hadn't seen hide nor hair of him since she was about nine. When she arrived at the hospital, she broke down quietly on the phone to Frank, who listened intently when she told him what she saw, in the bed, of what was left of Daniel.

Lilah called Ruthie, who took the bus from Lucasville to help care for Rosalee while Lilah stayed with Rose and Daniel. Ruthie felt somehow happy to do this for Rose, who had both taken away her husband and then given him back to her better than he was before. The reunion between Ruthie and Henry had produced a pair of twins that they doted on and would love until the end of time.

They brought what was left of Daniel home in a wheelchair and Rose prepared a bed for him. Her ink-black hair suddenly had streaks of white-gray and her eyes had hollowed. She rarely slept, but lay in her old place in bed alongside Daniel. If ever he thought he wanted to move a muscle, to seek a more comfortable position for his burns, Rose was right there to help him. Lilah had never seen a woman so devoted to a man, and she wondered if she had the same strength and dedication inside of her if something ever went wrong with Joe. Lilah pictured herself falling apart in times of disaster.

Rose cared for Daniel day and night, and she would never stop until she took her last breath or he took his, whichever came first. Taking care of Daniel became her religion—she let all else fall by the wayside, the way Lilah had let Henry's truck fall into the lake years ago. It was a good thing Lilah and Ruthie were there because all of the concerns of daily, everyday life—like paying bills and going grocery shopping—became their responsibility, along with Miss Jessie and the gang at the shop. Lilah paid for everything and Rose didn't know anything about it. She was glad to use some of the money she made for such a dear friend.

Night and day Rose prayed for Daniel to get better, to get up and walk with her, talk to her. But he didn't, he wouldn't, he couldn't. She could tell he felt her love, though; she didn't know how, but she knew it for sure. She felt weirdly distant with Rosalee, even angry inside. If this girl knew what was going to happen, why didn't she do something to stop it? Couldn't she have told Rose so she could have prevented the accident somehow? Rose never said anything about this, but Lilah sensed Rose's feelings toward her child. She wanted to protect them both, Rosalee from Rose and Rose from herself.

One night, Lilah heard Rose scream from the bathroom. When she opened the door, all she saw was blood everywhere. Mixed in were clumps of fetal tissue, pieces of the baby Daniel had prayed for and always wanted. Now, the baby was gone too. Rose didn't want to go to the doctor. She taught Lilah how to scrape her insides clean so that there would be no infection.

That night, Rose sat frozen in front of the television, wrapped tight in her bathrobe. She was numb. Lilah stepped in front of the TV and turned it off. She knelt down in front of Rose and looked up at her, supplicating.

"What you need, Rose?"

Rose considered the question. She could go on and list all the things that might lift her out of this thing, but she couldn't find the breath to make the sound and form the words. Finally, she just shook her head and let a lone tear fall.

She whispered, "Punishment. God punishing me for all the babies I let out years ago."

"God don't punish, Rose—"

"Then what?" Rose asked Lilah. Her eyes were dead and sad.

CHAPTER 25

AFTER THREE MONTHS WITH DANIEL AND ROSE, LILAH RAN home and threw herself into Joe's arms. She cried and cried and held him tight. She didn't know what on earth it would ever take to let go of him. He held her head in his hands and showered it with a million kisses, each one sinking deep into her face, her skin, her cells. Lilah felt every one of Joe's kisses fill her up, change her forever. It was that way in bed, too. It was as if all the years she had gone without sex reached out to Joe in the most primal fashion. Not that he was complaining! He took what she offered and returned it as hungrily as she gave. Before he met Lilah, he hadn't felt another person's need for him and only him. He had walked the earth with a fear that what happened with his first wife would happen again. He had preferred to confine his feelings to the safety of a little room on the bus. Now he felt the world break open, and he entered this new world inside Lilah's loins boldly. It felt like the safest place in the world.

Rosalee had changed after the foreboding feeling about Daniel's accident and Rose's miscarriage. She spent a long bout in the corner of the room in utter and complete darkness. No matter she was blind on the outside—there was darkness within now, too. For the first time in her life, she was aware that she could not see and she felt sorry for herself. She thought that perhaps Daniel was right, that she was missing things she would never see and the thought sent her reeling in a torrent of tears. Rosalee's blindness had never been an issue before, but she found herself torn up inside over not being "normal." The way she was, and even more, the way she was perceived by others, bought about a sense of loneliness she'd never known before. She wanted to get as far away from that strange part of herself that seemed to keep her apart from the rest of the human race. Her premonition was so awful that she sought to shed or bury this "gift."

Rosalee came out of this dark time determined to turn away from the magical places in her mind and concentrate on her working senses—tasting, touching, smelling and hearing. She occupied herself more and more with the things everyday sighted people could do: going to school, finding a job and then going to work, getting married, having a family. So that's exactly what Rosalee did, in exactly that order.

She met Walter at the Braille center she had started attending when she and Lilah returned to Memphis after the accident. She asked her mother and Joe to help her reach her goals. They found a good school in Memphis where she, quite literally, bumped into Walter when Joe took her in to register. It was a moment before the folks at the center noticed her; the sighted people were oohing and aahing all over Lilah and Joe, who was also a well-known entertainer, slapping his back and humming his songs and the like. A few of the folks asked Lilah for her autograph. Finally, they asked Rosalee questions about herself, how she got around without a walking stick and so forth. When she was demonstrating her "seeing" method for them, she just bumped into Walter—in the middle of the interview, just like that. It was like Walter was a homing device and Rosalee was his home. He cooed and cawed like one on the inside, too, when Rosalee finally finished with the registrar and Walter was able to get a minute with her. Joe waited in the car for Rosalee and let Walter make his move, securing his position in her heart for the next time she came into the center, which would be the next day. Walter was not shy—nope, not one bit. He knew what he wanted and seemed to know something or other about Rosalee's past without ever being told anything about it.

It went on that way with them for years until Rosalee was old enough and Lilah agreed that they could move in together. Rosalee and Walter were a blind couple, yes, but they were well-adjusted to the world and seemed to function almost as if they could see. Rosalee got pregnant quickly, and little cherubs who could see with their eyes were a wonder and a joy to their sightless parents.

Lilah was more than a little unsure how she felt about being made a grandmother so soon. She was young still—forty-nine— and had slowly inched herself off the stage and into semiretirement. Now that she was living full time in Memphis, she found out that her manager, Polka-dot Penny, indeed had a penchant for pennies—especially Lilah's. After the three months she lived with Rose, Lilah returned to find a lot funny business with getting more of the money she had earned. Lilah had lived off an allowance from Penny for years, ever since she signed with her and the record label. The stipend had increased as Lilah's popularity and record sales did, but she never really knew how much money she made over and above her draw and knew even less about the accounting of the money. She liked that it was there when and if she needed it—and it certainly came in handy during and after Daniel's accident—but she was content to spend whatever cash she was given weekly.

One day, Lilah looked in her purse at the drugstore and realized she didn't have any more cash on her to pay for the Twizzlers she liked to chew when she was stressed. Red ropes, she called them, lifelines for when you needed 'em. Twizzlers were Lilah's favorite candy. When she got home, she called Penny to let her know she planned to swing by for some more money, but Penny told her there was no more. There was no more money?

"What you mean?" Lilah asked, childlike. It was an honest question, but Penny ruffled at the insinuation.

"Just what I said. You don't have any more. You're broke."

"Well, where'd it go?" The question, again, was an honest one.

"Where does money ever go?" That was all Penny ever said on the matter, and it was the last time Lilah ever asked. Just as well. Lilah had been done with it all anyway—she was bored—and Joe's arms were the only things that held any interest for her. She found herself inside them more and more each day.

She and Joe moved in together but never married. She was content to be a has-been singer. Every now and again folks recognized her, but as time passed, the recognition was fading more and more, along with the color in her cheeks and hair. Lilah looked at herself in the mirror one day and a slightly graying, middle-aged woman stared back. She didn't feel the way she looked, and it was unnerving.

While Lilah was looking in the mirror at herself, frowning, the phone rang. It seemed somehow to be an insistent, urgent ring. This was important!

"Hello?" She braced herself.

"Lilah, honey, it's Ruthie." She exhaled. Ruthie's voice always made her want to do that.

"How you, Ruthie? The kids? Henry?"

"Everybody's fine, love." Ruthie's twin boys, Ray and Jay, were sixteen years old now. They looked alike, dressed alike and did everything together. They were gay and would later become staunch Southern advocates for gay rights.

Ruthie was silent a moment, and then she spit it out. "You gonna need to come on back to Lucasville."

Lilah drove up the long, dirt road that led the way into town. It was paved now, and in so many other ways Lucasville had changed. It became a sort of port of call for the area, a place where many places seemed to intersect into one. The paved street was now littered with cups and plastic bags from Piggly Wiggly, Staples, Kinko's and a ninety-nine-cent store. Lucasville had more people and cars than ever before, and Lilah marveled at the progress. She felt as if she had seen many lifetimes since she was here last.

Ruthie had called to tell her that this new computer company, IBM, was aiming to locate its headquarters in Lucasville and wanted to buy up a significant portion of the town for their offices and employee residences. Lilah and Samuel's house sat smack-dab in the middle of their proposed building site. Penny had paid the taxes on the house for years, but now... Almost all of Lucasville's residents—Honey Chile, Pop-Pop, Ruthie,

Henry, and the rest—had all received offers to abandon their homes and stores intermittently throughout the years by other companies—and they did—in exchange for sizable checks that would take care of their every want and need for the rest of their lives. Honey Chile came up with the great idea of pooling their earnings and purchasing an apartment building two towns away where they could all live together. Since she closed the store years ago, she finally began to mind her own business. Real estate happily took up much of Honey Chile's time. Pop-Pop was no longer interested in sex and that was just fine by her.

Lilah slowed to a stop when she got in front of her old house; it had stood empty for more than seventeen years. It was mostly the same, except more paint-peeled and dusty—not so much from the road dirt (they no longer had dirt roads in Lucasville) but from lack of use. She walked up the rickety stairs and onto the stoop where she found a red painted heart on the floor that read "Christie and Johnny Forever." She smiled. She was happy that another couple had taken up joy in the house she'd lived in and loved, with Samuel.

She fumbled in her purse for the key and opened the door. Beer bottles and McDonald's wrappers that travelers, squatters or vagrants had left en route to their final destination littered the house. She felt sentimental about the house, but not in a way that made her want to stay. It was symbolic of a time long past and she felt now *was* a good time to let it go. She turned and noticed a torn, yellowed picture of her and Samuel on their wedding day: Lilah was all flowing, gauzy white, and Samuel all starched for his young bride. The camera had caught one of the few inexplicably joyful moments of her life, as she remembered the feeling of walking down the aisle to become Samuel's wife. She knew that whatever time they had together would be full and it would be enough, though there wasn't a whole lot of people who agreed with her or saw things the way she did when she told them she was going to marry an old man. The picture captured the wedding-goers (her mama, her daddy, Ruth, Honey Chile and assorted townsfolk). In the distance, Nat was smiling and waving straight into the camera's lens, straight at Lilah now. She smiled at Nat's reflection, waved back, and blew him a kiss. She hugged the picture tight to her breast and turned to leave the house, but not before spotting her old friend Baby Girl's worn and tattered leash. She thought how nice it would have been for Lucky and Baby Girl to have met before each of them died; then she laughed aloud at the thought that, in doggie heaven, maybe they already had. That was all the tour Lilah needed. She signed the papers to sell the house to IBM and, two months later, received her check in the mail. The old house was to become another memory that would have to be kept in her heart and mind.

&

CHAPTER 26

ROSE HAD HEARD ABOUT THE CHANGES THAT HAD TAKEN PLACE in Lucasville—they existed as distant chatter in the furthermost corners of her mind. Daniel still clung to life and Rose never took her eyes off him but for more than a few moments—most notably, to get something to eat or drink, to go to the bathroom, or to do simple chores, the ones that couldn't go without doing. She hadn't noticed that the life-sustaining care she had given to Daniel all these years had compromised her own health. Rose felt her attention to him was what he needed to stay and be with her here, on earth, and she gladly gave every piece of what she had. Miss Jessie, ailing, stopped by every Sunday to leave a plate for Rose; Carla and Jolene took over Rose's managerial duties at the shop—they had learned from Rose all they needed as far as increasing their wealth. Shirleen had mastered the art and made enough money to escape Solomon. She and her two kids were safe in New York City with her family.

Daniel passed away quietly one afternoon, and Rose called Lilah and then Grace. They came, and so did many others, carrying plates of foods, with heavy hearts and wearing black. Burying Daniel, mercifully, was a quick passage for Rose, mostly because of the efforts of those she loved most. The day of the funeral, Grace had bathed her and Lilah dressed her.

Lilah started at her with a somber black dress, and Rose inched back. "What's the matter, Rose?"

"Don't wanna wear that." Rose didn't talk hardly much these days. Too many words taxed her energy, and since she had given her breath to Daniel for so long, there wasn't much of it to spare.

"How about this, baby?" Miss Jessie held in her hand the same dress and hat she wore the day she and Daniel got married.

She rubbed the dress against her body, caressing it as if it were Daniel. She moaned at the feel of the fabric on her skin, the warmth that the color gave off. Lilah hung the black dress back in the closet and Miss Jessie started to unzip the wedding ensemble. She opened the dress wide open so that Rose could slip her feet through—one after the other—while Lilah pulled it up and over her body. Rose had lost so much weight that the dress hung off her bones. She put the hat on her head, walked over to the mirror, and looked at herself. When she emerged from the bedroom and entered the living room, the mourners stopped what they were doing and quieted in a sign of respect for the person who most felt the loss. All that was heard was the *click-clack-click* of Rose's shoes on the hardwood floor as she walked across it to the front door and the waiting car outside.

The drive to the church was all of five minutes. Everything was a blur for Rose. What was left of Daniel lay before her in a box when she sat down in the front pew. There were some words spoken and tributes shared, psalms were read and hymns sung.

Afterward, the procession of people began. One by one they started down the aisle to shake her hand, give her a hug or a peck on the cheek. There were some who were there who hadn't ever met Daniel or Rose before, but had heard of their love and this woman's obsessive devotion to her husband. They wanted to lay eyes on this saint and pay their respects. Lilah sat on one side of Rose while Grace and Miss Jessie were on the other. Rosalee sat in the back pew with Walter, away from Rose, holding his hand and rocking herself.

Rose had received the grievers, but she never truly took one of them in. The last thing she remembered was sinking slowly into the ground and people rushing about her and then...blackout. Rose awoke, reclined, in the church's basement in the kitchen where the aroma of southern fried chicken floated thick in the air. People moved around her almost in slow-motion. There was not much she could recall, except the steady, insistent presence of Lilah, her friend Lilah, who wiped every tear from Rose's eyes. Rose regarded her friend and wondered if this was what she felt when her brother Nat passed. She cried a torrent of tears for Lilah's old pain, too.

Grace stayed with her Rose Ma awhile. There was no rush to get back. The election was over, she had won, and Frank went home to set up shop for his wife. Grace learned she was pregnant with their first child late one night when Rose was in bed, just lying there. Grace knocked.

"Come," Rose whispered.

"How you, Rose Ma?" Rose reached out to Grace and caressed her face. "I got something for you," Grace announced and removed a bag from behind her back. She took out a VHS, stuck it into the television, and pressed play. Dressed in her pajamas and wearing a ribbon—just like she did when she and Rose lived in Lucasville—Grace snuggled in bed with Rose and watched *The Wizard of Oz*. A beaming Judy Garland appeared on the screen. This time, though, she took up the entire size of the television, and the colors were bigger, better, and brighter. Technicolor. Rose looked over and smiled at Grace—her face hurt because it was so long since she had used those muscles around her mouth. Then she took Grace's hand in hers and held it tightly for the rest of the movie.

After that, time seemed to speed up. Speed up and away.

Months later, Grace brought her Rose Ma to live with her, Frank, and their newborn daughter Dora in Washington, DC. Rose often found herself serving as babysitter as Grace and Frank were often out at high-society functions. They were firmly entrenched as DGBs (Do Good Buppies)—young, educated Blacks with a social conscience. Rose was proud of Grace, though she seemed to be part of a generation she didn't always entirely understand. She couldn't for the life of her figure out how someone could drive a BMW yet fight for environmental rights with such zeal and self-righteous vengeance.

No matter. Rose was proud of what Grace had become. In fact, Rose credited herself with instilling in Grace a sense of her strength, the knowledge that she could do or be anything in the world she wanted to do and be. The next generation should always be better than the first—quicker, smarter, faster—and Grace was all those things. Grace juggled her career, her husband, and her family like most modern women, feeling the dual tugs of guilt when she wasn't spending enough time with one and joy when she was fully present with the other. Rose didn't envy the war between allegiance to work or family she saw in Grace, and she did everything she could to ease her burden.

While Grace was away at work, Rose stayed mostly in the house, cleaning and taking care of Dora. While Dora was asleep for her afternoon nap, she hungrily turned on the television to watch a succession of soap operas: the lineup started with *All My Children*, followed by *One Life to Live*, and then *General Hospital*. If Dora stayed down for a good long nap, Rose got to watch the *Oprah Winfrey Show* completely uninterrupted, which was a special treat. She liked that Oprah Winfrey and saw big things in store for her.

One day, she found herself trying hard to read a newspaper. When she brought the paper closer to her face, it seemed to get worse, but when she stretched her arms away from her face—ah! Relief! Rose could read the words! They were bright, crisp, and clear as a bell. Rose knitted her brow and remembered when she first saw her mother do such a thing—she was in her sixties then, like Rose was now. Rose was getting old and her eyesight was doing the things it had always threatened—or promised—to do to people her age. At first, Rose had a hard time accepting this. She went to the ninety-nine-cent store and picked up a pair of reading glasses to confirm if what she suspected was true. Maybe she had cataracts, or glaucoma or something like that? But the glasses were a big help to her reading. She hid her disability from folks at first, declining to read in front of others whenever she could. After losing the glasses, she went to the store and just bought up all they had and hid them in a bag in the closet.

One day, Rose helped Grace get ready for one of her buppi-fied balls. She wore a purple velvet gown embroidered with lace and organza to this one.

"This is beautiful," Rose admired as she helped Grace with the dress.

"It ought to be. This dress cost me one whole mortgage payment!"

"What?" Rose was aghast.

"Yes, Rose Ma. You have to dress to impress."

"Impress who for what?"

Grace laughed at her mother's naïveté. "Rose Ma! You just don't understand—"

"No, I don't and never will." Rose inspected the dress. It was a simple design, not complicated at all. Rose thought she could make that dress, too, if she had the right pattern, for a fraction of the price.

"Rose Ma Originals," is what she called the baby clothes she sewed for Dora. She went to the K-mart and bought patterns of the prettiest dresses she could find; she bought the fabric and stitched and sewed all day and all night until she felt confident enough to make her own patterns, her own designs. Rose was surprised to discover that she could do something creative and that she actually could be good with her hands! Wasn't nor never would be good at cooking—she surrendered herself to that—though she often felt a bit embarrassed by it, as if she weren't a real woman. She didn't have a great good need to really fiddle in the kitchen no how because Daniel was gone—nobody to cook for—and Grace and Frank preferred takeout and they always had food delivered to the house. Sewing was indeed a lost art, but it was found by Rose and it became her daily prayer, the one that helped her rise from the ashes and out of the dust of her grief. No one seemed to sew anymore, and when she told them that was how she spent her time, people looked at her with an odd mix of sadness and pity, as it revealed her age and how out of step she was with the rest of the contemporary world: the knowledgeable, cool and hip. Rose couldn't care less about what the "hip" people believed; she just didn't want her granddaughter to grow up thinking she had to spend her mortgage money to be accepted by people who never cared one bit about her in the first place.

Grace put the key in the door earlier than usual one day.

Rose perked. "Hey! You home early," Rose remarked.

"Rose Ma!" Grace seemed nervous. "Didn't expect to see you here!" Rose looked at her and knitted her brow.

"Where did you expect me to be?"

"Oh! Um—somewhere else, I guess." Grace smiled sheepishly. Rose looked at her—she was acting odd...

"You okay, Grace? You feeling sick or something?"

"No! No not at all!" Grace looked at her watch. "Rose Ma, would you mind picking Dora up from school?" Rose thought the request was a strange one, especially since the school bus let little Dora off in front of the house every day at 3:20 p.m. Rose knew this because she was the one who opened the door for her granddaughter who rushed in every day and smothered her face with kisses.

"Driver's off today. Everyone's gotta get picked up from school." Grace looked at her Rose Ma and smiled. Rose just looked at her—she couldn't for the life of her figure out what was going on, why Grace was acting so weird.

"Okay," was all Rose would say. She picked up her bag and was out the door.

Rose opened the school's big oak door. Dora went to Sidwell Friends, a private Quaker school. With their rolling lawns and stately buildings, Rose walked down the clean and shiny halls and marveled at the school's "Famous Folks," alumni who'd gone out into the world and made "worthy contributions to today's society." Rose thought about her own life and wondered if she had made any "worthy contributions." She wondered about all the other people who didn't go to fancy schools, and about the small ways they changed the world. Grace was Rose's finest accomplishment and she hoped that was enough to get her into the pearly gates and that all the terrible things she'd done in her life might one day be wiped clean and forgiven away.

"Excuse me, I'm here to pick up Dora?"

The woman behind the desk looked up at Rose and lowered her glasses.

"And you are?" She scanned Rose's body fully.

"Rose Johnson."

"But Dora's mother called and said her *grandmother* would be picking her up." The woman looked at Rose's body again with greater skepticism.

"That would be me." Rose looked the woman squarely in the face and thrust her hips forward. The woman lurched back a bit, uncomfortable with Rose's clear dominance and entrance into her personal space. There were more than a few things that cautioned the woman that Rose was not from these parts, so there would be nothing to lose by an altercation. It was Rose's fearlessness that made her pick up the phone and dial quickly.

"Dora's grandmother," the woman said as she looked at Rose's body a final time "is here." She nodded her head, then hung up the phone. The woman looked at Rose. "Dora will be right down, Ms. Johnson."

"Thank you." Rose looked at the woman one last time and walked away. The woman ogled the intimidating Rose and let her eyes linger longer than she would have gotten the chance to had Rose not stood squarely in front of her in that confrontational way she found so intimidating.

"Rose Ma!" Dora ran into her grandmother's arms and showered her with kisses, their usual style. Rose was at the point in her life where she decided she was completely open to receive love from a child, unlike the way she had been with Grace in the beginning. She was secretly proud of how far she had come.

"Did you have a good day?"

"Yes, Rose Ma! Look at what I drawed for you!" Dora took out a glued and crayoned, ratty piece of construction paper. On it was a heart with the words "Grandma Rose" inside and beneath it, a woman in a tight red dress. "That's you, Grandma Rose!" Dora pointed to the picture of the woman on the page and smiled proudly. "Teacher say no grandmother wears tight red dresses, but I told her my Rose Ma wore them and she was my grand-mother, so—" Dora shrugged. "Guess there was a grandmother somewhere who wears tight red dresses!"

"I guess there is, baby. I guess there is." Rose smiled. She smoothed down the child's unruly hair. Grace didn't take the time to brush it down the way she should. She said she wanted to instill in Dora a sense of pride and kept her hair natural, but to Rose, it was just plain nappy. Nothing Rose said would make Grace change her mind. Rose took Dora's hand and started again down the shiny glass hall.

"*Surprise!*" Rose and Dora opened the door of their home and found a cast of characters Rose hadn't seen in a month of Sundays! Ruthie, Honey Chile, Pop-Pop, Dice, Carla and Jolene (Miss Jessie was gravely ill in Newhope), Grace, Frank and some others beamed at her shocked face as she took all the folks in. "Happy seventieth, Rose Ma!"

"Oh!" It was all she could say. Rose had never had a birthday party before in her life. The only one she wanted to have—for her fiftieth—was virtually forgotten due to the effects of Daniel's bedside vigil. She felt something in her click on inside that was filled with gratitude that anyone thought enough of her to go to such extremes to celebrate her birth. Only Daniel had done it before with the simple sentence—*I celebrate your birth every day*—that made her rise the next morning to marry him.

It was a fish fry—Lucasville style—only it was enjoyed on the warm concrete of Grace's suburban DC terrace. Someone started playing a bluesy tune, and folks began to cut a rug right there in the middle of Grace's living room. Grace was happy she was able to do something for the woman who had raised her and loved her all her life. Despite her achievements in the world and aside from the birth of her daughter, Rose's surprise seventieth birthday party was Grace's proudest accomplishment. Grace watched as Rose hugged each and every person in the room, laughing and crying the whole while. Following Daniel's death, crying had become something Rose did freely and quite unabashedly—another great departure from the Rose that once was. Rose checked in with each of her guests, and she and Honey talked mostly about the building she and the others lived in that had just about tripled in value. Honey Chile was happy to report this news to all who wanted to hear and even to those who didn't. Ruthie was a passionate spokesperson of the Southern chapter of MOHK, Mothers of Homosexual Kids. Pop-Pop was retired and spent most of his time refurbishing old cars and looking at girlie magazines and Dice spent most of his time whittling it away in front of the television, playing solitaire and his namesake dice games.

"Rose Ma! We got one more surprise!" Rose clutched her heart—she didn't know if it could take much more of so much goodness. Out of the back room came a beaming Lilah and Joe.

"Happy birthday, Rose." She threw her arms around her friend and hugged her tightest. The crowd quieted down to a dull roar in respect for the longtime friendship between the women.

"We got something for you, Rose." Joe handed her an envelope; inside were three airplane tickets. "Lilah and me are going traveling and hope you'll join us to see the world. We want to see what the 'wonders' are all about."

After Penny had squandered Lilah's earnings, Joe gradually retired from the Hawgs and the Heifers. With his tightly kept savings, he made a series of shrewd and wise investments and became a financial powerhouse. He wanted Lilah to feel safe, like she would never want for anything in her life. But Lilah wanted little and needed even less than that, but she encouraged Joe to follow his dreams, trying out all the things he wanted to do in his lifetime: travel, have a ménage a trios ("Just once," he assured her, "but not with Rose!"), and cross through Darfur, Sudan, on foot and by bus. Lilah understood the part of Joe that wanted to be free because it existed in her too; only difference between the two of them was that Lilah knew she already was.

And so they went—Lilah, Rose, and Joe—and touched most all the corners of the world. The three of them had some of the best times of their lives while they were together on that trip, laughing, talking trash and eating the local food of the various countries and regions they visited. Rose never thought she would meet and see so many different people in all her life—she never knew they even existed!—but Lilah was less awed as she had experienced different people, places and things during her time touring. Joe seemed even more blissful and sublime than he usually was. He was always a quiet, happy man, but the love Lilah gave him sparked a new capacity to love he thought was dead inside. He often watched Lilah. Lilah would sometimes feel the heat of his gaze and turn toward him.

"What?" was all she could ask in response to his Cheshire-cat grin.

"Nothing. Everything!" He smiled, picked her up and spun her around. He thought to himself, *Life is full of surprises.*

Rose returned to her home in Newhope after their travels—Dora was old enough to let herself in the Washington DC house now. She arrived to find she had inherited both of Miss Jessie's Hair Bazaars and all of her wealth. Carla, Jolene and Mary had quietly buried Miss Jessie while Rose was away. Lilah and Joe went back to their sweet and simple life in Memphis.

One morning, Lilah awoke; the sun was unusually high in the sky. She lifted her head off the pillow and watched a single white butterfly make a stop on a sweet honeysuckle blossom outside the window before flying away. She smiled at the sight and wondered where the butterfly would be headed to next.

She looked up at the ceiling and mused aloud. "Joe, where you want to go next?" This traveling thing was exciting and fun. It wasn't her dream, but she took delight in seeing Joe's joy and sharing it. She didn't ever want it to go away. Not if it made him happy inside, which it clearly did. "Joe? Honey?" She turned over and put her arms around the love of her life. He was ice cold. Lilah jumped out of the bed backwards and looked at Joe's body, his back turned to hers. "No." She shook her head and looked at how still he was. She had never seen Joe that still. She inched further toward him and touched him again with her whole hand. "Joe." There was nothing. Just a cold, cold body.

"*Joe!*"

The doctors said Joe died of a heart attack as he lay in bed with Lilah. But only Lilah knew the real truth was that his heart was so full of love for her, one night it just burst wide open. That was all. Lilah never cried about it—she'd cried all the tears she had over death when Nat died years and years ago. The thing that held her up was the sentence the spirits uttered when Nat died. The spirits—manifested in the image and likeness of her daughter, Rosalee—said three words:

Dead, not gone.

So that's how it was to Lilah—Joe was dead, not gone. She often spoke to him aloud as she went through the busy parts of her day. Long and lengthy conversations, she and Joe had. It was an exercise that made the people around her uncomfortable, but she didn't care, not in the least. Then, Rose came and took her away, said she was going to live with her in Newhope, in the house they found together and squatted in almost fifty years ago. They would go there and live, live together until the end.

CHAPTER 27

THE ROUTE FROM MEMPHIS TO NEWHOPE WAS EXACTLY THE reverse of the trip she had taken with Rose some fifty years prior. Neither one of them had any business driving at all now, but they drove slow and careful and managed. Grace insisted Rose take her cell phone and call her twice a day to let her know where they were. Neither Rose nor Lilah wanted anyone to join them on the drive; it would just be the two of them.

"This is just like old times," Rose said as a tune oozed out of the radio.

"No, this one is different," Lilah said as she looked out the window at the setting sun.

"Why? How?"

Lilah smiled. "'Cause we both know where we're going to end up."

Their last day was a simple and quiet one. Rose and Lilah awoke. Lilah made some coffee, and Rose folded the laundry. The two were unusually quiet with each other, each leaving the other with room for her own thoughts. Lilah heard a noise in the bedroom and ran as quick as her old legs could take her. Rose lay on the floor and Lilah stared at her: there was no worse sight in the world than Rose dead. Lilah looked at her friend's lifeless body a while before finally picking up the phone.

"Rosalee? Rose is dead." Lilah made the statement evenly but with consideration. There was a knowing silence on the other end. Finally, the blind girl cried.

"Mama." The statement gave Lilah the permission she sought, the one a parent must have from their child before departing this world.

"Will you come?"

These were Lilah's last words before she hung up the phone. Lilah felt the desire to hold on—all living, breathing things seem to possess it—but it was only the most determined of those who taught themselves with intense practice, fortitude and will to loosen the grip and allow themselves to relax, let go, and *receive*.

Lilah saw the light, exhaled, breathed her last breath, and died. Out of her mouth flew a million of the most beautiful butterflies ever seen. The butterflies tickled Lilah and Rose all over their bodies—charming them—and then flew away en masse out the open door, as if being called by an external force.

It was Lazarus.

He walked slowly up the road, looking exactly the same as he had when he first appeared so many years ago. He smiled as he stopped and watched the butterflies rise up, up to the sun.

THE END